WHEN THE ACTOR INSPIRED CHAOS AND BLOODSHED

WHEN THE ACTOR INSPIRED CHAOS AND BLOODSHED

— A Novel —

NICHOLAS LITCHFIELD

Lowestoft
Chronicle
Press

LCP

Copyright © 2025 by Nicholas Litchfield

All rights reserved.

First edition: April 2025

Cover and book design by Nicholas Litchfield
Art credits include: iStock/CSA-Printstock

Print edition ISBN-13: 978-1-7323328-6-7

Library of Congress Control Number: 2024949556

Printed and bound in the United States of America

"A cinematic page-turner about Hollywood gone by, movie-making, and a throwback to a golden age of hard-boiled stories of noir and shadows, questionable morals, devious sins, and the unforgettable characters that made that world their own."
—CHRISTOPHER COSMOS, bestselling author of *Once We Were Here* and *Young Conquerors*

"Take ambition, greed, and a dash of corruption and mix them thoroughly on a movie set. Place it in a hot climate until boiling, and you will have the recipe for Nicholas Litchfield's entertaining novel."
—SHELDON RUSSELL, author of the Hook Runyan Mystery Series

*For Vivien, for the continual enthusiasm and for
motivating me to finish what I started*

WHEN THE ACTOR INSPIRED CHAOS AND BLOODSHED

DISASTER

MONTEVIDEO, URUGUAY
FEBRUARY 1997

Prologue

GUNFIRE rang out, dispersing the huddle of pedestrians congregating along the peripheries of the cordoned-off street. Blood splattered across the sidewalk, and the panicked movie executive gave a full-blooded shriek and clutched his left arm. The second bullet had found its mark, biting into the flesh just below his shoulder.

A split second before the handgun barked a third time, the executive dived to the ground like a stuntman might. The bullet smashed into the base of the Artigas Mausoleum, narrowly missing him, hitting the reinforced concrete with a sledgehammer thump, and earning another grizzly screech. His trembling hands moved to his head, forming a worthless shield, and he braced for impact, anticipating further gunfire, close to throwing up at the horrid prospect of a slug lodging in his spine. With his bloated face pressed to the ground, snot and sweat and tears clinging to it, his audible voice wailed a tune of grief and horror. *"¡Ayuda! ¡Dios mío! ¡Oh Jesús!"*

No matter how hard he prayed, the ground wouldn't part and offer some sort of makeshift crevice large enough to conceal his overfed body. He was done for—target practice for a hotheaded nutcase wielding a nice-looking shooter with rosewood grips that really caught the eye.

His terrified voice brought an immediate chill down Dominic Graves's back. Dominic, the film's star, the heroic lead in the macho picture *A Bullet for Silver Face*, was one of those rooted to the spot, his limbs momentarily unable to function. His terror-struck eyes plumbed the chaotic scene as the film crew scattered, and it was the sight of pedestrians running for cover that motivated him to flee the area. Self-preservation was at the center of his thoughts as he backed away from the gunman, but dumb confusion delayed him. He simply didn't know where to run.

"*Él va a matar a todos!*" someone yelled.

For an instant, Dominic's sight was obstructed by the blundering camera operator. The rotund man charged past Dominic like a demented animal, blocking the actor's intended path, and then he collided with the director of photography. The thumping sound of their bodies coming together was met with a muted groan, and the camera operator was immediately flung backward with stupendous force, landing on his ass.

Dominic caught sight of the boom mic hitting the ground and the operator scampering away. Then a hysterical man behind Dominic roared, "Run! Protect yourselves! Clear the set!"

The words leaped at Dominic like gigantic flames. Alas, the foolhardy actor rarely heeded warnings, and if he did wise up in time, chances were he would find himself running in the wrong direction and experiencing the full force of the explosion.

He knew he was doomed. He had always been doomed. He knew it the moment he inked his name on a contract with that serpentine agent of his, Bernie Finkelman. The man had made it his mission to steer Dominic into the path of danger. For decades, his incendiary words had caused harm and conflict, and the abhorrent way he behaved toward his clients was utterly incredible. He was a man who thrived on emptying an actor of his well-earned self-esteem. His joy in life was to bully, abuse, and undermine everyone he met. It was common knowledge that several fine thespians among his clients had made an unhappy exit from life too soon. One tumbled out of their fourteenth-floor apartment window, creating a messy splash; another used a shotgun to decorate his bedroom walls with his brains; a third died in his sleep, aided by a lethal stockpile of prescription pills. According to their files, it wasn't a lack of acting work that had diminished their lust for life, as each was regularly employed. Sadly, the work was far from impressive, and only the nature of their death brought attention to their obscure stage names.

Evidently, Dominic's demise would be even more remarkable. He was about to grab a headline or two in news outlets in the worst possible way: *Lead actor cut off in his prime.* Perhaps that was too optimistic. Mercifully extinguished for the greater good was more like it.

Dominic stared at the gunman, observing the crazed look in his maniac's eyes, and he found himself sobbing fitfully. He had lost control of his bowels already, and he was convinced that some of the lead in that pistol was headed his way. Which of his organs would remain intact and which would suffer horribly was all he could think about. Death and suffering seemed imminent, and the thought of it brought him to the verge of blacking out.

"Don't do it!"

The shouted plea momentarily kept the weapon from making another vicious sound, but soon, the finger closed on the trigger once more. The way that madman was brandishing his revolver, directing the little muzzle at the sniveling wretch on the ground, seemed quite expert. The fact that he had put a slug in the monument rather than the man suggested otherwise. Apparently, he was as inept with the gun as Dominic was with following directions.

But practice makes perfect, and there was plenty of ammunition in the guy's pocket to make damn sure he got the task done.

When the shooter steadied his arm, it was clear he had no thoughts of doing anything sensible, like putting down his firearm. He was beyond that, beyond reason.

The killing was about to begin.

"Bernie bloody Finkelman," whimpered Dominic.

Though he had only himself to blame, he preferred to put the blame squarely on his agent.

What the hell had compelled him to come to Uruguay to work on this disastrous mess of a picture? How had that venomous brute managed to charm him into throwing his life away for star billing on a two-bit movie nobody in his home country would ever bother to see?

Howling in despair and with tears cascading down his cheeks, he surged forward and then burst into a sprint.

True to form, he was headed in the wrong direction.

The shooter pulled the trigger again, and more than a dozen people screamed in dismay and sheer terror.

One

THE catchy R&B track on the radio offered Dominic Graves a peaceful distraction from his stressful morning commute to the gym. The speaker volume was low, but the sexy, softly sung vocals invaded his thoughts nonetheless. "My friends got their ladies/And they're all having babies/But I just wanna have some fun," crooned the singer, espousing the libertine existence. While not the upbeat type of music Dominic preferred, he had heard George Michael's latest song on the radio a lot and had grown to really like it. He raised his metaphorical glass to the singer and his prudent bachelor sentiments, muttering, "Chin chin."

The forgettable advertisement that followed the song served as a reminder that he hadn't had a decent acting job for weeks. The last thing he had done was a no-frills TV commercial for a car dealership. His last film role was in a tacky action picture where he had played a telegenic ex-Army Corporal-turned-PI investigating a missing American girl in Paraguay. Dominic was thankful he hadn't needed to venture beyond LA for any of the scenes. He hated everything about the picture and regretted not wringing the finicky director by the neck on his last day on the set.

He tried to shove the dour memories to the far reaches of his mind. That pain-in-the-ass director and his wretched movie had preoccupied Dominic's thoughts for too long. It was time to mull over something else for a change, something more cheerful.

Straightaway, an image of the splendid-looking Tibetan woman he had spent the night with popped into his head. Her white khata was so stupendously long that he had remarked it was like a bandage. Upon hearing her say it symbolized purity and compassion, he playfully rolled her over and, pressing his knee in the small of her back, wound the scarf around her wrists, fastening her arms securely behind her back.

A prickle of shame undermined his cheerfulness as he remembered her startled reaction. While she was face down on his mattress with her hands restrained, he had nibbled at her earlobe and whispered lewd observations in her ear. Though he intended only to tease and amuse, she had missed the funny side of his actions, and his knavery sent her into a frenzied state of panic.

At the time, the act had done quite the reverse for him. He had never felt more aroused. Now, he felt like a contemptible brute.

He let out a doleful sigh. It was a debauched way to behave. *You're becoming more and more like your father, you bloody cad*, he acknowledged with a sorry shake of his head. *I'm the one in need of restraint. The girl deserved better.* He squinted as he tried to recall her name. It was a useless exercise. He was sure he hadn't asked her what it was, and if she had offered that tidbit of information, it would have been immediately forgotten. *Let's name her Tibet, after her country of origin. The perfect little name for such a sweet, pert creature.* A deplorable, crass grin instantly materialized as he recalled her exotic, feminine magnificence, but guilt and a desire to atone for his beastly conduct wiped the smile away. The memory of her squirming helplessly on his mattress would stay with him for a very long time. Concern that this unpleasant experience might impact her future relationships weighed heavily on him. *Why did I think it was worth it*, he asked himself?

Throughout his twenties, he was guilty of habitually seizing opportunities for mild sexual mischief, never apologizing or making amends for any harm he may have caused. Having entered his thirties, he slowly began to allow empathy and respect to enter his consciousness.

His small, sleek Motorola StarTAC cell phone shuddered in the cup holder, offering a further distraction. Leaning forward slightly, he took his eyes off the interstate for scarcely a few seconds to peer down at it. The phone was rarely out of his reach, and for the past month, he had used it relentlessly, but this was the first time today it had made a sound. Eager for conversation, he snatched up the vibrating clamshell phone, careful not to drop his newest high-priced gadget. The light, slender thing cost more than all the dreary, timeworn garments in his meager wardrobe, and it was more fashionable than anything he had purchased all year.

His eyes widened with optimistic zeal as he flipped it open and saw his agent's number on the display screen. To put it mildly, he was desperate for work.

Just as he was about to answer the call, he observed the truck ahead of him swerve into his lane in a belated attempt to reach the off-ramp. He slammed his foot hard on the brake, but he was going so fast it didn't make much difference. His eyes zoomed in on the bumper sticker on the truck as his car hurtled toward it. He was so close he could read the words: BRAKE NOW…OR YOU'LL BREAK SOMETHING. There wasn't time to heed the advice. A split second before his bumper made contact with the sticker, he swerved violently to avoid the truck and slammed head-on into a road sign.

He heard a thud and then a sharp crack as the sign crumpled his bumper, flipped over the hood of his car, and smashed against the windshield. He stared in shock, watching the sign fall away. It didn't dawn on him until much later that the airbag in his sedan hadn't deployed. He remained in his seat for several minutes, trembling fiercely, gripping the steering wheel so tightly that his knuckles turned white. The truck continued without stopping, and traffic went by him, indifferent to his accident. Eventually, he felt his pulse return to normal, and he got out of his car to inspect the front of the vehicle. Although the scratches and dents bothered him slightly, he wasn't so vain that he cared much what people thought of the car he drove. The shattered windshield did trouble him, though. The glass was massively cracked, and the driver's section was partly falling in.

He got back in the car, hunched down in his seat, and, pressing his feet against the windshield, began to hammer at the glass with the soles of his shoes. He didn't stop until he had kicked the front windshield out. He breathed with relief when the glass fell away.

Immediately, he pulled himself upright in his seat and speedily got back onto the interstate. The heavy pour of whiskey in his morning coffee kept him from reporting the accident.

Twenty minutes later, he dropped off his vehicle at his usual garage, relieved he had made it there without getting pulled over by the police. While he sat in a rigid chair in the waiting room, anticipating a long wait while the mechanic assessed the damage, he checked his cell phone's voicemail and was pleased to see that his agent had left him a message.

Bernie Finkelman's hoary voice rasped in his ear: "It's now eleven thirty AM. Figure you must still be in bed, huh? Boy oh boy, what a life you lead. Your day begins at noon when you roll out of bed, and the nights don't end until dawn, right?" The old man sighed long and hard. Dominic pictured him rolling his eyes and silently cursing him.

"You haven't had any acting work for a while now, so you're prob'ly depressed. Prob'ly been hittin' the bottle hard and prob'ly taking your frustration out on some unlucky schmuck naive enough to take you up on your offer of a free drink. The poor sucker had to listen to you rant and rave all evening about what a sensationally gifted actor you are and how wretched it is that you haven't got a half-decent agent who can hook you up with those good movie parts you deserve. Christ! If I got a nickel every time someone spouted that horseshit, I'd have enough loot saved up to retire." He made a noise almost like a growl, then mumbled incoherently. Dominic kept listening to the message, wondering what the phone call was about.

"I just hope, for your sake, you got a quality forty winks at some point during the night, kid. Or was the whole night a grueling slog of drug-induced hallucinatory hell? I know how you are with those pills and powders you love to turn to when things aren't going your way. Your actor buddy, Kurt, told me all about those flophouses you sneak off to late at night. There's always something disgusting going down in those fleapits, and I'll bet you're at the center of the most sordid activities." Bernie chuckled condescendingly. "Didn't think I was aware of your dirty shenanigans, did you? Yeah, I know a lot of your dark secrets, Dom. You're the least discrete person I know. Get help, kid. I'm sure it's just a matter of time before we start seeing needle pricks all over your arms. With any luck, the police will raid that drug den sooner rather than later. Either way, it'll end in tears, mark my words. And I won't grieve for you. Other than a toothless old whore, and perhaps an out-of-luck drug peddler, no one will mourn your passing." He stopped ranting to blow his nose into a handkerchief. Dominic listened to the unpleasant sounds of abundant snot discharging from his nostrils.

"Not sure if I should tell you this, but I had a premonition this morning that someone discovered your bloody corpse in a parking lot, shoved in a dumpster. The police were labeling it a drug deal gone bad. The locals were insisting it was environmental cleanup." Dominic could sense the enjoyment in Bernie's voice. "What a way to go, eh? You might have no memorable movies in your portfolio, but your life would certainly have a memorable ending."

He cackled, highly pleased with himself. Dominic didn't find it the least bit amusing.

"Anyway, when you finally get out of bed and check your messages, give me a call. I have a job you might be interested in. I'd like it if you got back to me about it sooner rather than later.

I have plenty of other decent, grateful clients who would jump at this opportunity. Call me or swing by the office."

A smile finally found its way onto Dominic's face. Getting an earful of ridicule and criticism from his agent didn't seem so bad now. Possibly, it meant that the man was in fine spirits this morning. A brief, lackluster message might imply that the old man had lost interest in him, which may spell the end of their long union.

Dominic shook his head, thinking how ridiculous that sounded. How could an agent-client relationship get so totally twisted? It hadn't started well, and it had worsened steadily over the years. Bernie always had snide things to say to him, but these days, the man didn't even try to conceal how he felt about his client. He was repulsed by Dominic. Viewed him like he was some sort of genital wart. Dominic wasn't overly fazed by Bernie's abhorrence of him, and he was so used to listening to the man's offensive remarks that he wasn't rankled by them anymore. This latest message, however, was slightly different from the norm. He detected a great deal of urgency in his agent's voice. Figuring the job opportunity must be a good one, he immediately called back.

"Bern, this is Dominic. I'm returning your call. I'm at the garage, getting my car fixed—"

Bernie instantly cut him off. "I don't have time to chit-chat, kid. Skip breakfast and get down here. I want to discuss a movie part with you."

Dominic raised his eyebrows an inch. "A movie part!"

"Yes. A good one, too. I'm in my office until one o'clock. Get here by then, and we'll talk about it over lunch."

"Didn't you hear me, Bern? My car is at the shop. Hello? Hello? Bern?"

He swore indignantly and pounded the arm of the chair with his fist when he realized Bernie had hung up on him. The actor's facial muscles hadn't had this much exercise in weeks.

Two

DOMINIC exited the taxi and entered the office building just after one o'clock. He made his way sluggishly up the ten flights of stairs to his agent's top-floor office. He was breathless when he reached the top step. Sweat stains showed through his white cotton shirt. Bernie Finkelman's office door was wide open, so Dominic went straight inside. The old man was still at his desk, slouched in front of a noisy fan. He was attempting to read the newspaper, but the whir of the fan was lulling him to sleep. Dominic observed Bernie's eyelids flutter and his head continually bobbing back and forth as he desperately tried to stay awake. Evidently, it was getting near the old man's naptime.

Dominic walked across the room and sat down in the rickety wooden chair beside Bernie's desk. "You had lunch already?" he asked casually.

With a startled yelp, Bernie reached for his Windsor cane.

"Whoa. Hold on there, slugger," said Dominic, throwing himself back in his seat and putting his hands up. He nervously eyed the hefty brass handle on the man's walking cane. "It's just me—Dominic—your number one client."

"Christ!" muttered Bernie, quivering with shock.

He lowered the cane, propping it against his desk, and then put a trembling hand to his craggy face, covering his eyes with the palm. After taking a few deep breaths, he took the hand from his face and said bitterly, "You scared the crap out of me, kid. I coulda had a heart attack. You ever heard of knocking?"

Dominic jerked his head, gesturing toward the open doorway. "Your door's wide open."

"So?"

"You wouldn't have heard me anyway. Your fan's too loud, and you're too close to it to hear a thing."

"Bullshit. I coulda heard ya. There's nothing wrong with my ears."

Dominic found himself staring at the old man's ears, which looked absurdly large compared to his smallish head. He remembered reading somewhere that some Chinese consider prominent earlobes propitious. The bigger they are, the more prosperous you are. Some men actually have cosmetic filler injected into their earlobes to make them longer. The idea appalled him. He could understand breast or penis enhancements, but voluntarily making one's ears larger sounded idiotic. If there was a way to stop them from continuing to grow naturally as a man ages, perhaps that was a procedure worth the investment, not the reverse. While he studied his agent's drooping earlobes, which hung like he had worn heavy earrings for much of his life, he wondered what the Chinese community would make of the man. Were his earlobes big enough to suggest he had a small fortune tucked away in the Cayman Islands? Then he glanced at the grimy collar of Bernie's pink and blue striped shirt. A sneer made its way onto his face. So much for looking prosperous, he thought. If his clothes were anything to go by, the man had exhausted his funds in the early 1980s.

Bernie noticed the contemptuous look on his client's face and grunted with annoyance. "In future, you knock," he said, pointing a threatening finger at Dominic. "Or I'll teach you some manners."

Dominic held his tongue. Conversations with Bernie were typically unfriendly. "Get out and go to hell!" That was how the old man generally spoke to him, and that line was usually his closing remark. He was well aware that Bernie had a low opinion of him. It wouldn't matter how successful he became; he was sure that Bernie would always treat him like dirt. So why was he still with that hoary monster, he wondered? He couldn't stand the man; he hated having to deal with him but felt tied to him for some reason.

When Dominic moved to LA five years ago, out of work and with limited acting credits to his name, he was bounced from one talent agency to the next so stiffly that his ego got bruised. Eventually, he paid to attend a casting director workshop, and that's where he met Bernie. Dominic was so desperate to forge a career in Hollywood that he was willing to sign up with any agent. Bernie's tepid remarks didn't fill him with much joy. "I don't see star quality in you, kid. Your talents might be better spent working in a fast-food restaurant, but you have a great set of teeth and a smile that might lure a casting director to the couch."

Those comments were good enough to win Dominic over. He scratched his signature over Bernie Finkelman's coffee-stained contract and prayed he had done the right thing.

Days after signing on with Bernie, Dominic's auditions improved, and TV work came his way. Dominic didn't know if Bernie had opened doors for him or if talent had gotten him where he wanted to go. Either way, joining forces with Bernie had turned out reasonably well for both men.

"So, what's this great part you called me about?" said Dominic, getting straight down to business.

Bernie shuffled some papers on his desk, taking his time to reply. His hands were still visibly shaking. When he lifted his head, Dominic detected resentment in his flinty blue eyes. "Forget about it, kid. The more I think it over, the more I'm sure you're not right for the picture. I should never have called you; I don't know what made me pick up the phone. It's all these damn prescription pills I'm taking. They're playing havoc with my emotions. I must have been caught in a brief flash flood of pity when I phoned you."

Dominic slammed his fist down on Bernie's desk and said angrily, "Hey, I busted my windshield trying to take your call."

"You did what?" Bernie examined him as if he were insane. "What the hell did you do that for?"

"I didn't do it deliberately. I had an accident. I swerved into a road sign on the interstate."

Bernie looked horrorstruck. "Damn crazy. Did you hurt anyone?"

"No."

"That's one good thing. You shouldn't be taking calls while you're driving. It's downright dangerous. There are enough reckless drivers on the road without you adding to the numbers. Where's your car now? You drive it here with a broken windshield?"

"No, it's at the garage. I had to get a taxi here."

"Prob'ly for the best. Leave it at the garage. Lousy drivers shouldn't have cars."

"Bastard," muttered Dominic under his breath. He was sorely tempted to give Bernie a little whack on the head with that mean-looking walking cane the old man carried. "I'm here now, aren't I? And I'm soon to be out-of-pocket nearly three hundred bucks. If there's an acting gig going, I want to hear about it. What's the part?"

Bernie sat back in his chair, studying him coolly for a moment. "Very well," he said, finally relenting. He slid open his desk drawer and pulled out a slim, spiral-bound movie script. "It's a thriller set around a technical college. As you can see, the script is nice and short, just how you like 'em," he remarked, tossing it to Dominic.

The screenplay zipped across the desk and landed in Dominic's lap before he could grab it. When he picked it up and started to leaf through it, his eyes lit up. "This is a feature-length movie, right?"

Bernie gave a nod.

"I'll give it a read while I'm on the treadmill this evening. Should be able to get through the whole thing during my workout."

"Jules Fern at Griffin Pictures thought you might be a decent fit for the part of Bruce Pucker."

"Oh yeah? What's this Bruce guy like?" he asked optimistically. "The studious sort? Teaches Latin and Greek? Likes to translate Catullus and Ovid in his spare time? Not sure I like the name Bruce. Can it be changed to Nathaniel?"

"There'll be no changing of anything," said Bernie irritably. "This Bruce character isn't a professor; he's a news reporter. Drinks so much that, half the time, people assume he's just a dumb, loudmouth jerk. More brawn than brain. You know the type. Thinks highly of himself, lacks manners, upsets people. A bit of a lothario but always disappoints in the bedroom. You should have no trouble playing the part. You'll have to beef up your muscles, but otherwise, you're a perfect fit."

Dominic groaned. "Why do I always get these roles, Bern? Can't you find me something better? How will I ever show off my acting chops if you keep fixing me up with shallow characters?"

"Count yourself lucky to get any scripts," grumbled Bernie. "That pretty girl, Jules, is looking out for you. God knows why."

He eyed Dominic suspiciously, wondering if something had happened between them at the Christmas party Griffin Pictures had hosted the previous year. Bernie had heard rumors about a short-lived affair but never found out if the stories were true.

"This is a talking part in a movie, and it comes with a paycheck. You should thank your lucky stars that this script found its way into your grubby hands, not bicker about it."

Dominic looked down at the script, feeling disgruntled. "*A Bullet for Silver Face*," he muttered, reading the title page aloud. "Catchy title. Sounds like a real winner."

Bernie nodded, the hint of a grin showing. "Just your shot of whiskey, Dom. A group of corrupt police officers in Uruguay are involved in an arms trafficking ring. They're preying on smugglers, bandits, illegal aliens, and local criminals, procuring weapons, then selling the stockpiles to Brazilian criminal organizations—"

"Uruguay!" interrupted Dominic. "Doesn't sound very believable. Shouldn't it be set elsewhere? I can think of plenty of other countries where these shady goings-on are far more commonplace."

"Sure," admitted Bernie, "But as these crimes happen in all sorts of places, why always stick to the same old locations. Anyway, Uruguay happens to be a pretty good venue. Arms trafficking doesn't have its own category of crime under Uruguayan law. It falls under 'trafficking illicit contraband,' which is a lesser crime. So, Uruguay isn't such an unlikely setting. Border control between the two countries is very lax, allowing for all sorts of trafficking. It's conceivable that Brazilian gangs could be situated in Uruguay, operating from within."

"Fine. What does the title have to do with the story?"

Bernie sifted through the jumble of folders on his desk. Jules Fern had faxed him a summary of the movie plot. The relevant crumpled document, half-hidden under his newspaper, was smeared with jam from his morning donut. He brushed off the sugar, licked his fingers, and then read aloud the pertinent details.

"A Border Patrol agent is gunned down at night when he confronts a large group of bandits. Before he dies, he takes out one of the gang members. The others get away. However, one of the suspects, nicknamed 'Silver Face,' is later apprehended in Montevideo. He's in possession of firearms that were previously involved in a government operation called Mission Gunroom." He looked fleetingly at Dominic to see if he was still paying attention. "That's the moment when Bruce Pucker comes onto the scene. He's a reporter for *USA Today*, sent there to nose around, sniff out the truth. There's a strong suspicion that the government is involved in a cover-up. The official story behind the shooting keeps changing; there are many inconsistencies and denials. Very quickly, there are lots of people with tight lips and lots of stonewalling going on in the case. The suspect in custody is married but has a troupe of women he likes to hang around with. One of these girls, María, owns a chain of beauty parlors and teaches beauty therapy at a college. She has connections with dozens of unsavory people. Bruce ferrets around, trying to learn as much about her as he can. Eventually, it leads somewhere, and he breaks the scandal wide open."

Dominic rolled his eyes. "I think I've seen this movie before."

"Good. Then you'll know exactly how to play the part."

"I guess. You'd better fill me in on more than just the story. Where are they shooting this one? And what sort of budget are we talking about?"

"It's all shot in Uruguay." He sensed Dominic was about to object and fluttered his hand to silence him. "The movie has a fairly big budget attached, Dom. Well over two million. It's not just Uruguay money that's financing it. The dough comes from Argentina and Germany, as well. It'll be a good opportunity for you to get some exposure overseas. And if this picture does well, it could do wonders for your career."

"How long's the shoot?"

"Ten weeks. Plus a few extra days for reshoots." Again, he put his hand up to hush Dominic. "You'll fly out in January, which is the warmest month. You'll be back home by late March when the rainy season hits Montevideo."

Dominic rubbed his chin contemplatively. He still wasn't entirely convinced he wanted the part. "What's the director like? Is he any good?"

"Ignacio Martinez. A very smart and knowledgeable man, I hear. Good work ethic, very charming, knows exactly what he wants."

"Is that your polite way of saying he's a tyrant, a bullshitter, and a control freak?" said Dominic warily.

Bernie started to nod but managed to stop himself just in time. "I haven't met the guy. I'm sure you'll love him, especially when the gross receipts come in and the awards are handed out. He's an insatiable man, apparently. Likes his food and his women in equal measure. And he's thirsty for success. Think what a successful picture could do for your career." He rubbed his index finger and thumb together, saying, "Get on well with Ignacio, and he might cast you in his next movie. I smell money, Dom. Thick wads of Ben Franklin and Will McKinley, maybe some Grover Clevelands, as well."

"I guess it could be a good stepping-stone for me," said Dominic, thinking of the busted windshield on his car. "You really think he's got a big career ahead of him? What else has he done?"

"He started out young, by all accounts. Did some good short movies while he was a student, then a low-budget horror movie that he executive produced when he was twenty-one."

"By twenty-one, huh? Not your average student, then," muttered Dominic, envious of him. "I guess the program wasn't challenging enough."

His eyes clouded as he thought back to his own university days, enrolled in the BFA program in Acting at Syracuse University. He had hoped to follow in the footsteps of notable alumni like Frank Langella and Peter Falk. Never mind technique or text analysis, creative improvisation, voice, speech, and movement—for the most part, his days consisted of excessive drinking, skirt-chasing, and little else. By the end of university, *his* one proud achievement had been the rudimentary act of completing his degree program and earning a diploma.

Bernie's reedy voice invaded his melancholy thoughts. "He taught film at a college for a while, then formed his own company and produced and directed TV shows. A couple of years ago, he made a popular independent movie that won some awards in Uruguay. That was his second feature film. I think he's also done some music videos and worked in special effects. I don't really know, though. I'm just guessing. He's been around for a while and turned his hand to a lot of varied things."

"Has he only worked in Uruguay?"

"I think he may have worked in Brazil and Argentina, but I'm not sure. I know he's got connections in many South American countries."

Dominic's eyes narrowed. "How did he get such a big bankroll for this picture?"

"Who knows?" said Bernie, throwing his hands up. "Frankly, who cares?"

"Sure, what does it matter?" mumbled Dominic, convinced that drug money was funding the picture. "If there's so much dough going around, won't they want one of their own boys playing Bruce Pecker?"

"Pucker," corrected Bernie.

"What's an American doing in it, anyway?"

"I think Ignacio wants to appeal to North American audiences. Jules told me a slew of American actors were approached to do the part. They all passed on it. I heard a story that Jay Adler-Frankel flew out to Uruguay to meet with the director and gave a good reading. He signed the paperwork and was set to do the movie. Then they had some sort of falling out."

"Over money?"

"No. Well, maybe," said Bernie, mulling the question over some more. "I couldn't get the full story. All I know is that while Jay was in Uruguay, he got into a car accident. Totaled a Porsche 968 Turbo RS."

"Is that an expensive car? How bad were his injuries?"

"Of course it's an expensive car! Very fast, very glamorous, rather rare. Noisy as hell, mind. Jay walked away from the accident unscathed. Didn't have to pay a nickel toward the damage, either. It all sounds very strange. Too strange, if you ask me. You know how these publicists are—spin all sorts of wild yarns for a living and do whatever they can to pump some interest into their clients' flagging careers."

Dominic grunted in agreement, recalling some of the wacko stories he had read about certain celebrities. There were a fair number of absurd rumors floating around about Jay Adler-Frankel. When he wasn't drunk and disorderly, threatening his neighbors with his pet boa constrictor, or getting into fistfights in bars when drinking duels involving absinthe cocktails got out of hand, he was shooting his mouth off on live television and grabbing crude headlines in lowbrow newspapers for his extramarital affairs with midgets. The British press, in particular, couldn't seem to get enough of him, and for the longest time, he was a regular feature in their tabloids. Although they had plenty of disreputable characters—hell, Parliament was full of cranks and crooks—for some reason, they loved to devote vast amounts of column inches to ridiculing Jay.

It was difficult to gauge the impact of all this negative press on the actor's career. Did he benefit from the overseas exposure, or did it harm him? As far as Dominic could tell, it made no difference to the actor, whose private life was so fraught with misadventure that he had little time to focus on his career. One might argue that Jay's movie career was all but over anyway. The last Dominic had heard of him, he had checked into a rehab clinic.

"Wish you knew more about what happened," mused Dominic.

Bernie shrugged. "Doesn't really matter, does it? He's out of the picture, and you're next in line."

"Yeah, why is that, exactly?"

Bernie chuckled. "Bizarre, isn't it? They say it's all because of Jules. Various names were bounced around to play the lead, and she dropped your name into the conversation. Nice move on her part, as it turned out. Strangely enough, the director had heard of you. Can you believe that? He saw you in *Bolivian Hound*—liked what you could do with a gun. Apparently, he's partial to the tough, gritty actors who perform love scenes with blood trickling down the side of their face."

Dominic's face twitched with irritation as he recalled his bruising experience. He had been thrown around by irritated henchmen most of the time. The little matter of the fracture to his jaw during an on-screen fight scene bugged him the most. As he recalled his unhappy experiences, he muttered, "My character isn't involved in any fistfights, is he?"

Bernie gave a vigorous shake of his head, muttering, "A few, but nothing major."

"What do you mean, *nothing major*? I don't want to become a human punching bag again."

"It isn't anything like *Bolivian Hound*. Christ! What a beast of a movie! That director...bah!" He shook his head ruefully. "Turned out to be a real sadistic pig, didn't he? If I'd known what he was going to put you through, I'd never have let you do it. Not for that paltry amount of money, anyway."

"After that whack to my jaw, I could hardly deliver my lines, Bern. The empanadas were bad enough without choking on a knuckle sandwich as well. I need this face for acting, dammit!"

Bernie was in complete agreement. His client's good looks were his chief selling point. Practically his only selling point.

"If this is another slugfest, I'm not doing it," Dominic said sternly. "You're supposed to be an acting agent, not a boxing manager."

Bernie forced a smile, although there was displeasure behind his eyes. "You got it. Give the script the once-over tonight, and let me know if you want to do it. I really think this is your shot, Dom. This is the picture that will open doors for you, and not just in South America. Can I expect a call from you tomorrow?"

"Sure. I'll call you when I get up."

Bernie scowled at him. "When you get up! Humph. So, in the late afternoon, then?"

"Or thereabouts," admitted Dominic with a carefree shrug. Then, with a faint sneer, he added, "By sunset, for sure."

"Fine," said Bernie, looking disgruntled. "Now get out and go to hell!"

ADJUSTMENT

MONTEVIDEO, URUGUAY
JANUARY 1997

Three

DOMINIC stood in the baggage claim area of the gleaming, spotless Carrasco International Airport, fantasizing about clean sheets and a firm mattress. The flights had been too long, and the San Salvador and Lima layovers were not long enough. It was now five thirty in the morning. A full day had dissolved while he had been cooped up on planes.

He rubbed his eyes while he waited for his luggage, wishing away his headache, thoroughly regretting having guzzled alcohol during the second flight. He hadn't just had a tipple with his meal, either. That wasn't his style. He had glugged down beer like he was celebrating his birthday, and now his tongue felt as rough as his brown ostrich skin shoes.

He straightened his back, hearing bones crack. Sitting inert for hours had wreaked havoc on his muscles and made him feel like a haggard old man. Even his chic beige suit looked shambolic. Now profoundly wrinkled, it bore unsightly stains in several places; he couldn't determine what had caused the brown blemishes but figured the filthy marks would be tough to remove. *Did turbulence make some of that bourbon find its way onto my suit jacket*, he wondered?

His grubby appearance contrasted with the clean-looking airport, which was so fresh and chic that he wouldn't have been surprised to see cellophane wrap on the equipment.

"Bingo," he muttered, finally spotting his bag on the carousel.

A vintage olive-green suitcase on wheels, made of Italian calfskin leather, stood out among the other drab luggage. He had bought it for a modest sum of money at a flea market on the Quai Jean-Charles Rey in Monaco with some money he had won in a casino. The rest of his winnings had paid off his extravagant hotel bar tab.

He found a sudden burst of energy and scurried over to grab the bag off the rotating belt. Exiting the airport, he went straight to the taxi rank outside. He couldn't wait to get to his hotel and go to bed. He planned to sleep for twelve hours straight. Nothing would disturb him—he had brought enough sleeping pills to stock a pharmacy.

The cab driver instantly got out of the cream-colored Mercedes-Benz and took hold of Dominic's luggage, admiring the leather suitcase quietly before placing it in the trunk. Dominic slid into the back seat of the car and took a slip of paper out of his pocket with the address written in block letters. When the driver returned to his seat, Dominic said, "Take me to Hotel Casino Carrasco. I have the address written down."

"I know where it is," said the driver.

Nevertheless, he took the slip of paper from Dominic and glanced at it before driving off.

"What's your opinion of the hotel?" asked Dominic. "My agent insists it's good, but he's about as honest as a Chicago politician. I'd prefer to know what a local thinks about it."

"I recommend it highly, señor. It's a luxurious hotel. Historic. Dates back to the early nineteen hundred. The palace on the sand, they call it. A magnificent building to look at. I think you will enjoy the views from your room."

"I'm supposed to be in a suite that overlooks the beach."

The driver glanced at Dominic in his interior mirror. "You are fortunate, señor. If you have the money, a suite at this hotel is an excellent way to spend it."

"My employer is paying for the room," clarified Dominic,

wanting to quash the idea that he was well-off. He wasn't planning on tipping well.

"The best money to spend is somebody else's," the driver said with a wide grin.

The journey from the airport took about fifteen minutes. When the taxi pulled up at the hotel, Dominic handed the driver twenty bucks. "Keep the change. You can have a drink on me."

The taxi driver's eyes gleamed at the sight of the dollar bills. "Thank you, señor. I will drink for us both."

"I might want you to drive me around tomorrow," said Dominic as he got out of the vehicle.

"*Sí*, señor." He stepped out of the cab and shoved a crumpled card with his telephone number into Dominic's hand. "Call me. I will come immediately."

Dominic glanced at the card before he pocketed it. "You got it, Gonzalo."

The driver got Dominic's bag from the trunk while Dominic gazed across the road, past the palm trees, at the shimmering blue water beyond. He was idly wondering how hectic the filming schedule would be. The temptation was to spend the morning exploring the neighborhood and perhaps get a little sun in the afternoon while relaxing on the beach. He told himself that whatever happened, he would make time to enjoy the Carrasco barrio before he left Montevideo.

Gonzalo handed him his bag, and Dominic thanked him and lugged it to the hotel doors. The doorman, elegantly attired in a brown and black suede frock coat and white gloves, opened the door for him. When he stepped into the large, marble-floored lobby, he was impressed with the opulence that confronted him, from the chic outfits of the hotel staff to the enormous crystal chandeliers and beautiful stained-glass ceilings. He hauled his luggage to the reception desk, feeling slightly rueful he hadn't asked Gonzalo to do it.

"I have a reservation under the name Dominic Graves,"

he told the receptionist as he searched various pockets for his passport. Having shown it to airport personnel so many times throughout the day, he was now uncertain where he had put it.

He wasn't sure of the duration of his stay. Filming was supposed to end sometime in March, but the possibility of reshoots convinced him he would remain a while longer.

He eventually located his passport in the front pocket of his bag. The receptionist smiled warmly at him as he handed it to her. He hadn't noticed how attractive she was until he had seen that smile, and while she searched her computer for his reservation, he admired her smooth, tan face and long, auburn hair, which extended to her waist.

"I see your reservation, Mister Graves," she said, looking up from her computer screen.

"Dominic," he insisted.

"A room is reserved for you for the next ten weeks, Dominic."

He gazed favorably about him at the elegant décor, pleased by his surroundings. His lodgings were rarely this nice. The production company had spoiled him.

The receptionist placed a glossy little map in front of him and explained the various facilities in the hotel, and though he nodded, he wasn't really listening to her. "Enjoy your stay here, Dominic," she concluded.

"I'm sure I will. I just hope I have time to enjoy the spa and casino."

"Also, I have a package for you." She collected a thick manila envelope from the mail slots on the wall behind her and handed it to him, along with the key to his room.

"Thank you. Incidentally, I was told I would be in a suite."

"It is a standard room."

He gave a slight groan and wrinkled his brow. "I guess one room is as good as another."

"Let me see if there is something I can do about it," she offered. "Please give me a moment."

While she turned her attention back to the computer, her long fingernails tapping the keyboard noisily, his eyes roved her body again. He was a man who, where women were concerned, appreciated all varieties—particularly those, like the receptionist, who had a tremendously fulsome figure.

"Actually, there is a suite available," she said at last, "but it would only be for three nights. You will have to move into a standard room on Thursday. Would that be acceptable?"

"That would do nicely," he said, beaming. He tossed the key to his standard room onto the desk, murmuring, "You've just made my day."

"Enjoy your stay," she told him, passing him the key to his suite.

The key, shiny and new, seemed to sparkle with lavishness, and he put it in his pocket and walked away, feeling a little less apprehensive about his stay in Montevideo.

———◆———

The suite was roughly twice the size of his apartment in LA and far more appealing. He looked around at the expensive antique furniture and the large paintings on the walls. An enormous bed with a canopy around it seemed excessive and out of place yet exquisite and enchanting.

He parked his suitcase by the sturdy baroque wardrobe and tossed the manila envelope on the bedside table. Then he took off his shoes and flopped down on the inviting bed, intending to relax for a few minutes. He had been told to call a woman named Maria as soon as he arrived at his hotel. She was the director's personal assistant. It seemed that the director liked to keep her schedule full. Before Dominic left LA, she had apologized to him in advance for not intending to send someone to meet him at the airport. She was too busy running errands for the director.

Dominic was too tired to look in his suitcase for her telephone number. Truth be told, he wasn't particularly motivated to contact her, still peeved that he'd had to find his own way to the hotel. This sort of treatment might cause another actor to have low self-esteem.

He glanced at the telephone on the bedside table, goaded by the sight of it. Now that he found himself horizontal on the comfortable bed, he convinced himself he was too drained of energy to do much at all. He let his heavy eyelids rest and drifted into a state of unconsciousness. Within a matter of seconds, he was lightly snoring.

Alas, all too soon, an incessant chime close to his ear startled him awake. He rubbed his eyes and sat up, uncertain of his surroundings. Sunlight streaked through the blinds, illuminating his room. He realized the telephone on the bedside table was calling out to him. Making a sudden lunge for it, he managed to get his hand to it in time.

"Hello?" he said into the receiver.

"Dominic? This is Maria Romero."

"Ah, yes, I was about to call you," he lied.

"Did you have a comfortable flight?" she asked mechanically. "You find the hotel easily enough?"

"Yes, yes. All good."

"You didn't call me. I was worried something had happened to you." Her tone was absent of concern; in fact, she seemed rankled. "The director would very much like to meet you this evening. He wants to go over some of the scenes for tomorrow."

Dominic groaned inwardly. "We're shooting scenes tomorrow?"

"Yes. There's been a slight change to the shooting schedule. We begin early. Six o'clock."

"Six in the morning!" said Dominic, trying to keep his voice steady.

"There are a number of scenes to film. You have the information packet I left for you at the reception desk?"

Dominic looked at the unopened manila envelope on his

table next to the phone. "Uh-huh. Got it."

"It has everything you need, including the call sheet for tomorrow. Ignacio hopes to finish by ten o'clock, but there's a strong chance that everyone will need to work through the night to keep from falling behind schedule."

"Christ!" he muttered solemnly. "He's having me pull an all-nighter on my first day on set."

He dreaded to think what the rest of the shooting schedule would be like. So much for lazing about on the beach, he brooded.

"There a problem with that?"

The bellicosity in her question surprised him. With great effort, he managed not to take up the fight. "No, no problem," he replied bitterly.

"Good to hear. We want to start off on the right foot, don't we?"

Take a breath, he reminded himself. *Unclench your buttocks and be professional, dammit.*

For a moment, he found himself actually trying to work his sphincter muscle in the hope it might make him less uptight. He wished the caustic Maria Romero might do the same.

"What time does Ignacio want to meet for dinner?" he placidly asked.

"Eight o'clock."

He thought it encouraging that he was meeting the director in advance of filming, even if it was only ten hours in advance. He made a mental note to exercise some restraint during dinner. It was imperative he didn't knock back the drinks like he had done earlier during his flights. Allowing the director to see him shitfaced—particularly during their first meeting—was something even Jay Adler-Frankel might frown upon.

"Where should I meet him?"

"Go to the hotel restaurant. I've reserved a table for you both."

"Wonderful," he said, trying to inject some enthusiasm into his voice.

"Welcome to Montevideo," she said as something of an afterthought. "I look forward to meeting you properly tomorrow."

He thanked her and replaced the receiver. Then he studied the clock on the wall, puckering his brow when he realized it was almost midday.

He grabbed the bottle of Ambien off the bedside table and tossed a pill in his mouth, helping it down with a tepid glass of water. Was it wise to take one so late in the day, he wondered?

To hell with it, he decided. Jay Adler-Frankel would absolutely approve.

Hours later, the persistent jingling cry of the phone nudged him out of his extended sleep. His eyelids fluttered open, and he automatically rolled onto his side and reached for the chunky telephone on the bedside table. "Who is it?" he croaked into the receiver.

The husky, unfamiliar female voice was clear and concise and all business. It was seven o'clock in the evening, partly cloudy, and a pleasant seventy-five degrees Fahrenheit. She then recommended dining in, as the cuisine offered in the hotel restaurant was something to cherish. Laundry service was available to him should he require it. The stranger's deepest yearning was for Dominic to have a joyously peaceful evening and make full use of the exemplary amenities the hotel offered. And for now, that was all she wanted to say.

He slammed the receiver down, annoyed by the automated message but thankful he wasn't late for his meeting. He had a full hour to make himself presentable, and boy did he need it.

He unzipped his suitcase and took out some clean clothes, which he tossed on the bed. Then he grabbed his leather toiletry bag and went into the bathroom. When he looked at his reflection in the mirror, he was dismayed by the haggard face that stared back at him. There were dark circles around his lifeless gray eyes, and his youthful skin looked sallow and flaky.

He filled the washbasin with lukewarm water, rubbed hand

soap on his face, and took a fancy-looking straight razor with a three-pin horn handle from his toiletry bag. After exposing the high-carbon steel blade from the handle and admiring the splendor of the implement, he got to work. He had watched countless movies where a barber skillfully shaves his customer, so he was well-educated in terms of grip and technique, knowing to keep his ring finger hooked over the tang, place his thumb on the side of the blade next to the center, and rest his middle and index finger on the back of the blade. He knew to hold the blade at a thirty-degree angle and, using even strokes and very slight pressure, move the edge in the direction of the grain. He knew to stretch the skin with his other hand and keep it taut.

Unfortunately, though he was an expert in the theory side of things, when it came to the practical side of shaving, he was more like a butcher than a barber, and minutes later, blood dripped from various nicks on his face and neck, making it look like a vicious tomcat had mauled him. He grabbed a styptic pencil from his toiletry bag, wet the tip, and pressed it against each of the cuts for a few seconds. Then he daintily applied some cream foundation to cover the blemishes. He stared at his reflection, proud of his handiwork yet aware that a makeup artist would curl her lip at the sight of him.

He didn't allow himself much time to dress, and it was precisely eight o'clock when he exited his room. His taupe pants and white shirt looked like an unhappy combination, and the deep creases made him look worse.

Thank God for my overwhelming good looks, he thought. Looking as he did, one might forgive him for almost anything. Maybe even murder.

Four

WHEN he entered the elegant hotel restaurant and gave his name to the maître d', he was immediately escorted through the vast oval dining room to a table by the window. Ignacio Martinez was already seated. A soft peach-colored blind was drawn, and a decorative lantern hung over his suave face. He was engrossed in a leather-bound book, which turned out to be the menu, his finger smoothing the hair on his pencil mustache.

"Mister Martinez, thanks for inviting me to dinner," said Dominic, standing over him.

Ignacio promptly pushed his menu to one side and quickly got to his feet. "Dominic Graves, the great American actor," he said, his voice deeply accented. "The next Hollywood heartthrob. And this director's new muse. Finally, we meet in person." His eyes flitted about Dominic for a few seconds, quietly admiring his physique, before adding, "You're even more dashing in person than you look in the movies. What a supreme smile you have. It's a movie star's smile. One that can lure the prettiest of women into bed." He gave a filthy snicker.

The man's offhand adulation threw the actor off-guard. He didn't know quite how to respond. Smiling politely, he mumbled, "I wish."

This was a rare instance where he felt valued and deserving of his headlining role. Though still unseasoned, he had appeared in enough pictures to know his way around a set and anticipate a few rough encounters. Most directors welcomed him with civility, but he seldom detected sincerity in their smiles. Some gave him the impression they were doing him a favor by casting him in their picture. Ignacio was something else entirely. His warm words bordered on toadying, and the enthusiastic compliments made Dominic anxious. Though desperately wanting to live up to a director's expectations, the actor doubted he ever could. He had convinced himself that the quality of his acting would be judged differently in this unfamiliar country. It was first a matter of deciphering the new metrics and then a case of working to meet the standard. Did he have the aptitude and versatility for the task?

It was a question that would keep him up at night for weeks to come.

Ignacio leaned in, one hand clasping Dominic by the wrist and the other taking his hand firmly. The handshake was strong and energetic. Too spirited for Dominic's liking.

"We're blessed to have you in Uruguay," Ignacio murmured with a troubling look in his eye.

Instantly, his grip intensified, sending shooting pains through Dominic's arm. Dominic gritted his teeth, fighting back agony, trying not to let his discomfort show.

As the director pumped his hand, Dominic stared hard at the man, wondering what was really going on behind those brown, twinkling eyes. Did Ignacio secretly despise him?

It was a long, agonizing greeting, and all the while, Ignacio smiled and muttered kind words to him, but the man's smile was off-putting, his teeth looking like something from a horror film. Dominic stared at him, mesmerized, unsure what to make of this unexpected detail. There were distinct gouges in Ignacio's front teeth. Marks that ran deep in the enamel. The strangeness of these grooves reminded Dominic of a fascinating article he had read in an anthropology magazine reflecting on curious ancient practices of mutilation. Weird, unnecessary dental work trended throughout the world from 700 to 1400 AD, with deep horizontal furrows chiseled into the enamel across the upper front teeth. Whether decorative or a status symbol, nobody seemed quite sure of their purpose. Likewise, the severe blemishes on Ignacio's teeth represented another baffling mystery that Dominic was hesitant to bring up in conversation. Were the marks the result of a freak accident? Perhaps a modern badge of courage harking back to the Viking Age? The notion that they might, in fact, highlight that he belonged to a particular cartel made Dominic keep his thoughts to himself.

"I've been looking forward to our dinner together ever since you agreed to do this movie," Ignacio said in Dominic's ear, seemingly unaware of his own strength and the queerness of his front teeth.

He let go of Dominic's hand and cackled like a lunatic. Then, he gave the actor a playful pat on the cheek before inviting him to sit. Dominic tried to appear unruffled, which was far from easy. His fingers hurt, and his eyes were watering. He glanced down at his aching hand, noticing the bright red blotches on his skin. Flattery and courteousness aside, Dominic suspected that beneath the jovial veneer, Ignacio was, at heart, a vicious, insensitive brute. *God help me*, he thought, contemplating what was in store for him during the next ten weeks. He muttered a few words of gratitude and then sat down, discreetly massaging his tender hand under the table.

"Thank you, Favio," Ignacio said to the maître d' who was still hovering over Dominic's shoulder.

Favio, who had patiently waited for the men to take their seats, now handed Dominic a menu. In a thick accent, he promised them both an exceptional culinary experience and slinked away.

"What do you think?" asked Ignacio, his cinnamon-brown eyes glimmering as brightly as the mass of crystal chandeliers that lined the ceiling.

Dominic frowned at him. "About what?"

"The hotel. Isn't it a lovely restaurant?"

"It's exquisite," said Dominic, glancing about him. "I can't thank you enough for putting me up in such a beautiful place. My room is terrific, and the restaurant looks dazzling."

Ignacio nodded, gratified by the remarks. "We're blessed with some of the finest hotels. This is one of my favorites. I filmed a scene in this restaurant two years ago." He slapped his hand on the wooden tabletop with unwarranted force, frightening Dominic. "At this very table, in fact."

Dominic gazed at him apprehensively. He glanced quickly at those seated nearby, surprised that nobody in the restaurant seemed disturbed by the man's eccentric behavior.

Ignacio prattled on, oblivious to Dominic's unease. "The owner is an incredibly gracious man, so generous and helpful. He was very excited about his hotel being used in the movie and went out of his way to accommodate the film crew. We filmed extra scenes in the lobby and the kitchen. Actually, we employed a lot of the hotel staff as extras. The maître d' you met just now, he had a small speaking role." He smiled fondly, thinking back to the experience. "I love it here. I'm pleased that you like it also, Dominic. I want you to be completely relaxed when you're not on the set. Enjoy the spa, enjoy the casino, and take advantage of as much of this as you can."

Dominic was in complete agreement. He fully intended to live like a monarch for the next ten weeks.

"When you work hard, you deserve the luxuries that come with hard work," said Ignacio. "That's my philosophy."

Dominic examined the director pensively. The phrase "hard work" often scared the hell out of him. His thoughts went back to the nonstop filming frenzy of his very first film, *The Burning Choice*. The awful monster movie was shot in three days—an impulse movie by a shoddy director who had just finished shooting a movie ahead of schedule. The director made use of the expensive set by filming a second picture in the three remaining days he had left. Though Dominic admired the man's initiative, he found his taste level questionable. The script was hurriedly written, the actors chosen almost at random, and time was so limited that, frequently, there wasn't the chance to do a retake.

Ignacio saw Dominic give an involuntary shudder and mistook his reaction for hunger pangs. "Forgive me for talking so much. You must be ravenous after such a long and hectic day."

He gestured to the menu in front of Dominic. "The food is wonderful. The hotel specializes in French cuisine, and the chef is remarkable. What are you in the mood for? Meat? Fish? Eggs?"

Dominic fingered the menu nervously. "I'm in the mood for meat."

"What sort of meat?" He watched Dominic hastily scan the menu. "Beef? Lamb? Chicken?"

"Lamb sounds good."

"In that case, may I recommend *le gigot qui pleure*," said Ignacio, tilting his head to read the menu in Dominic's hand.

Dominic glanced at him inquiringly.

"It's called a 'crying lamb gigot.' The meat is slow-cooked in the oven on a grill, with the potatoes underneath on a rack. The juices from the meat drip on the potatoes as they cook."

Dominic could feel himself salivating as Ignacio described the cuisine. "Sounds delicious."

"It is. I remember…"

He lost his train of thought at the sight of the waiter arriving at their table. The waiter was exceedingly fat, and his manner was patently distracting for both men. He stood very close to them, his stomach protruding over the table, his chest pushed out tremendously. His chin was in the air, and there was a supercilious look on his face. Ignacio seemed more amused by him than annoyed. He ordered the same dish as Dominic and was all for letting Dominic choose the wine. Unfortunately, Dominic was having difficulty selecting something from the comprehensive wine list. Ignacio watched him glide his index finger across the menu as though he were painting with his finger. He could sense by the glazed look in Dominic's eyes that the man's finger was unlikely to come to rest on a satisfactory wine.

"If I may," he advised. "Chateau La Lagune is a fine choice of wine."

He waited patiently for Dominic's approval. Dominic's knowledge of good wine was as sophisticated as his knowledge of French cuisine.

"Nothing too dry for me," Dominic told him.

He then fumbled the menu. It dropped into his lap and slid to the floor, causing him slight embarrassment. The waiter let out a perceptible groan as he stooped to pick it up. He had difficulty staying on his feet while groping around under the table.

"Then I think this will suit your palate," said Ignacio, unfazed by the incident. "It is a fine Bordeaux wine. Rich, sweet, and full-bodied, but not too heavy."

The waiter straightened up, wheezing slightly. His face was red, his eyes bulging. He gave an approving nod. "A red Médoc wine will complement the lamb."

"In that case, yes. It sounds good to me," said Dominic.

The waiter gathered their menus, scowling at Dominic, and slowly strolled away. Dominic was relieved to see him go.

"You like French cuisine, Dominic?" asked Ignacio.

"I tend to eat in Italian restaurants."

Ignacio gave an understanding nod. "The most popular food, and the most straightforward to prepare. There are only four to eight ingredients in a typical meal. Me, I am a fussy eater. I like rich foods. Food with plenty of flavor. Meals serve as satisfying moments in my day. When my taste buds have been stimulated, I feel enthused. Think of all the preparation that goes into an excellent meal. All that hard work and fine craftsmanship. How one treats their food reveals a lot about a person. Are you the sort of man who barely looks at what is on your plate? Do you gobble it up without thinking about how it tastes? Are you paying more attention to your glass of wine than the food on the end of your fork?"

"More often than not," admitted Dominic guiltily.

"Some foods naturally command our attention, of course," continued Ignacio. "Personally, I value food as much as I value my time. I want it to be a pleasurable experience. French cuisine fulfills that need."

"You put people like me to shame. I eat merely to fill up."

"Your body will thank you if you fill up on delicious food rather than pasta and bread. William Cowper said it best: 'Variety is the spice of life.'"

The waiter came by their table with a bottle of wine. He uncorked it and began to fill their glasses.

"My assistant, Maria, told you about tomorrow?" asked Ignacio charily.

"About the early start?"

"Yes. I want everyone on set by six o'clock at the latest." He politely nodded to the waiter, who set the bottle on the table, bowed slightly, and left them alone. "I apologize for such an early start. I know you must be exhausted after your long journey. I cannot help it, unfortunately. We had some setbacks last week that put us behind schedule. I simply cannot let us go over budget."

"You've had problems on set?"

Ignacio nodded somberly. "Heavy winds blew down part of the small set we built, and it also stopped us from shooting some of the in-flight scenes. Then the aerial photographer fell out of the plane." He paused to sample the wine.

"Jesus!" muttered Dominic into his wine glass. "Is he dead?"

"No," said Ignacio with slight displeasure. "He only broke his arm. It happened before the plane took off. He slipped and landed awkwardly and needed to be sent to the hospital. It meant altering our schedule until he returned. This we were able to do. However, the scenes he filmed when he returned were not good

About the Author

Nicholas Litchfield is the author of the novel *Swampjack Virus* and editor of twelve literary anthologies. His stories, essays, and book reviews appear in various magazines and newspapers, including *BULL*, *Colorado Review*, *Daily Press*, *Pennsylvania Literary Journal*, *Shotgun Honey*, *The Adroit Journal*, *The MacGuffin*, *The Virginian-Pilot*, and *Washington Square Review*. He has written introductions to numerous books, including twenty-one Stark House Press reprints of long-forgotten noir and mystery novels. Formerly a book critic for the *Lancashire Post*, syndicated to twenty-five newspapers across the U.K., he now writes for *Publishers Weekly*. You can find him online at nicholaslitchfield.com or Twitter: @ NLitchfield.

enough." His monstrous grimace pronounced his contempt for the man. "He is in pain whenever he holds the camera, which has caused problems getting the scenes shot properly. Now we are behind by several days."

"You think you'll be able to get back on schedule after tomorrow?"

"No," sighed Ignacio. "If we start at six o'clock every day from now on and cram additional scenes into each day, we might just get there."

Dominic tried not to show his discontent. It was clear that he would be put through his paces for the next couple of months. He doubted there would be time to enjoy the casino or spa. In fact, he'd be lucky if he found time to enjoy his hotel bed.

"When the film is done, you will thank me for pushing you so hard," Ignacio assured him. "You get out what you put in. Don't you agree?"

Ignacio was turning out to be the continual idiom dispenser.

When the waiter brought their meals, Dominic's mood lightened. He could smell the food before it arrived at their table. He eyed his plate with intense hunger.

A dreamy expression appeared on Ignacio's face as he retracted the fork from his mouth. "Heavenly," he murmured with his mouth still full.

The waiter took the liberty of refilling their wine glasses before he walked away from their table.

Ignacio dabbed at his mouth with a napkin. "I'll introduce you to the cast and crew tomorrow. I hope you didn't think I was intentionally rude by leaving you alone for most of the day. I figured you would want to spend time by yourself, relaxing after that long flight."

Dominic thanked him for being so considerate. He didn't fully believe Ignacio, though. It seemed more likely that the director simply couldn't be bothered to have someone meet him off the plane.

"How's the food, Dominic? Better than the Italian meals you like to fill up on?"

"It's divine. I see now that I've been missing out on good food all my life."

"Make sure you leave room for dessert," Ignacio advised. "The profiteroles are the perfect way to finish this dinner."

Dominic slurped his wine, grunting appreciatively. He had a sweet tooth, and anything that paired cream puffs and vanilla ice cream with hot chocolate sauce was the ideal way to conclude any meal.

Ignacio didn't say much for the rest of the meal, choosing to concentrate on his food. Toward the end of dessert, he noticed his lead actress, Sofía Prodova, sitting at the bar. He pointed her out to Dominic.

She was pretty, with short, curly hair. The hair was dyed blond, and the roots were hardly showing. She was sitting on a barstool alone, nursing a large brandy. The captivating way she sat on that stool made Dominic's eyes bulge. She couldn't have looked lovelier in her tight red dress, which helped to show off her splendid bumps and curves. To those around her, she was a perpetual distraction. No red-blooded male could have had any complaints about the length of her dress. Every time she shifted in her seat, the little material would ride up her thighs, giving Dominic a fantastic look at her impeccably toned legs.

Ignacio watched her admiringly. "Perhaps you will get to meet some of the cast today, after all."

Dominic pushed his empty plate to one side and glanced back at Sofía, licking his lips. "I'd like that very much."

"Let's join her for a nightcap."

Five

WHEN Ignacio tapped Sofía lightly on the arm and asked her if she minded having company, her glossy lips broke into a delightful smile. After a brief but tender hug, she guided him onto the stool beside her. Those round, cinnamon eyes of his concentrated on her with the same fascination as they had the dinner menu. Ignacio didn't seem able to break eye contact with her. He appeared to have forgotten Dominic altogether, making the actor feel like a discarded understudy.

"My God, you're positively ravishing tonight," the director told her, slavering like a famished canine.

He was full of lust, his hands trembling slightly, resisting the longing to paw at her. With a crooked forefinger, he summoned the barman over.

"What would you like to drink?" he said.

Although he was addressing Dominic, he didn't make it clear, and the actor stared blankly, failing to respond even when the director frowned at him.

"The way you drank your wine made me think you were thirsty for more," muttered Ignacio.

"Oh, me," said Dominic with slight embarrassment. He saw the snifter glass on the counter in front of Sofía and found the color of the liquid appealing. "I'll have the same as the lady."

"A good choice. I'll have the same."

Ignacio gave a curt nod to the barman, who was adept at

following his customers' conversations, whatever the language. Tossing his bar towel over one shoulder, he automatically began preparing their drinks.

Ignacio's eyes darted back to Sofía. "Darling, I'd like to introduce you to Dominic Graves."

"Ah, the American…you're here already!"

She swiveled in her seat with surprise and examined Dominic as if he were a newly acquired museum piece. Her eyes observed every stray hair and tiny wrinkle on his face. She seemed most fascinated by the broadness of his shoulders.

"My flight touched down this morning," he mumbled.

She shot an angry glance at Ignacio. "I wasn't told Dominic was arriving today."

The director smiled contritely. "I'm sure I mentioned it to you last night, dear."

"No, you did not."

He tilted his head to one side, his smile widening. "Are we sure about that?"

"Yes, we are sure."

"You did have a lot to drink last night," he said scornfully.

She threw her head back and chuckled, making light of the comment. "I had a few glasses, yes. Not so much that you should make an issue out of it. You'll make Dominic think I'm some sort of boozehound."

The sneering expression on Ignacio's face made it clear how he felt about her drinking habits.

She delicately got off her stool, somehow managing not to let her dress ride further up her legs. "Welcome to Montevideo."

The friendly embrace, open and intimate, felt most inappropriate. Her chest was pressed against his, her arms wrapped around him, warmth and passion and familiarity in her grip. The hug was that of a lover, and it had no rightful place during this initial meeting.

The director's audible groan added to the awkwardness. It was full of frustration and disappointment.

Dominic looked up and noticed Ignacio was a little close for comfort. His hands were on his hips, his chest jutting out like a prizefighter readying for a face-off. The man's stern expression signaled that Dominic had displeased him.

It was then that Dominic realized his folly. His impious hands had drifted to Sofía's rear, and it looked like he was testing the ripeness of two large peaches.

He extracted himself quickly, stepping back, wanting to apologize for his roving hands but too embarrassed to acknowledge his loutish conduct.

"I've heard so much about you," Sofía said, overlooking his indiscretion. "I almost feel like I know you, Dominic. Filming started a while ago, and it felt strange working with all the cast members except for the main actor."

Ignacio surveyed his actor discontentedly. Dominic's groping hands had shocked and irritated him, and he was wary about what the actor intended to do next. "She's been asking incessantly about you," he muttered unhappily. "I have told her everything I know."

"Nothing but good things, I hope." The old cliché tumbled out of Dominic's mouth naturally, but he instantly regretted saying it, not wanting to give the allusion that there were plenty of bad personality traits.

"Sit," said Ignacio, slightly barking the request.

Dominic parked himself on his stool, sitting on command like a dog before its owner. His throat was dry, his mouth eager to taste more liquor. He wasn't sure what to do with his hands. To his horror, when Sofía returned to her seat, she seemed to drop her left hand in his lap. He kept his eyes on hers, pretending not to notice, hoping the director hadn't, either.

She genially patted his thigh. "I saw one of your movies. Bolivian Dog."

"*Bolivian Hound*, I think you mean," corrected Ignacio sulkily.

"I thought you looked wonderful in it. Ruggedly handsome and very charismatic. You gave quite the performance."

Dominic thanked her, wishing he would hear flattering things like that more often. It felt even more gratifying coming from the sweet, shapely lips of a pretty actress. "I had no idea that movie was so popular over here."

Sofía and Ignacio exchanged furtive glances and then burst into laughter. Dominic shot Ignacio a questioning look.

"Not the case," confessed Ignacio, trying to control his mirth. "The movie was…how do you say…a turkey. I believe that's the correct term you use in America."

"I see," said Dominic, rather crestfallen.

Ignacio shrugged apologetically. "You were good, don't get me wrong. You did what you could with that ghastly script, but it was always going to be a total failure. You can't turn a piece of crap into something finer. It is what it is. Tell me, did you read the script and think it could be something special?"

Dominic's eyes roamed the bar while he tried to recall his initial feelings after first reading it. He remembered having difficulty learning his lines and stumbling over much of the dialogue. With a dismissive shrug, he said, "I don't remember what I thought. It was a busy period for me. I was too scatterbrained at the time to know much about anything."

"But why did you do the film?" persisted Ignacio.

"My agent told me to do it."

"Aha, as I suspected," said Ignacio, clearly amused. "You did it for the money. We're all guilty of that. Money dictates most of the things we do, but what stops us making the big turkeys," he said, wagging a chiding finger, "the ones we suspect will turn out to be complete crap, is the fear of what it will do to our careers. One dud picture can spoil our job prospects for the next one. Isn't that so?"

Dominic nodded somberly.

"Anyway, you were not to blame. What on earth could you

have done to rescue it? It was beastly. Fetid. And from what I hear, VHS sales stank as well. On the positive side, the movie gave us all a good laugh, never mind that it was supposed to be a drama."

He gave a short, mocking laugh.

Dominic managed to keep his emotions in check. He wasn't a fan of the film, but it was never pleasant to hear others ridicule any of the few movies he had made. He said evenly, "How come you both saw it? Was it widely distributed in Uruguay?"

Ignacio shook his head. "No, no. I have a copy of the movie. I put on a special screening for the cast and some of the crew. I thought it might be useful."

"Useful? How so?"

"I knew that by the time you arrived in Uruguay, we wouldn't have as much time as I usually like to set up shots. Seeing how an actor moves and hearing how he delivers his lines provides the film crew with a mental picture of what to expect."

Dominic looked at Sofía with doubt in his eyes. "Did *you* find watching it useful?"

"Oh, yes," she insisted. "I knew nothing about you before I flew here to do this picture. When I watched your movie, it eased my mind about you."

The waiter set a glass of brandy in front of Dominic. When Dominic picked it up, Sofía's glass clinked against his. "*Sah lood!*"

"*Sah lood!*" repeated Ignacio, raising his drink.

Dominic smiled politely and raised his glass. "Cheers."

For the next hour, they chatted affably, with Dominic deliberately steering the conversation away from his previous movies. Eventually, Ignacio suggested they all get some sleep.

"I'll send a car to the hotel tomorrow morning to collect you both. Please be waiting in the lobby at five-thirty sharp."

Dominic wanted to look at the script again before going to sleep, but he also wanted to make sure he got adequate rest.

"Goodnight," said Ignacio, slapping a hand on Dominic's

shoulder, the force of which almost caused the actor to tumble out of his seat. "Sleep well."

He kissed Sofía on the cheek, murmuring in her ear. She shook her head and indicated she wanted to finish her drink. He courteously bid her goodnight, though with a nasty grimace, then exited the restaurant.

Sofía twisted around on her stool until she was directly facing Dominic. "I know you must be exhausted, but would you mind if we ran through the script together?"

"It's as if you read my mind."

"I don't feel ready for our scenes tomorrow. I feel like I need another day to learn my lines."

"I feel like I need at least another week."

Sofía raised her eyebrows in silent agreement and took a short swig of her drink. "I don't want to keep you up all night. I just want a short run-through of tomorrow's scenes."

"That's fine with me. We can spend as long as you need. I had a nap earlier."

When he lifted his glass to his mouth, she tapped him lightly on his knee and said, "I've left the script in my room. I'll go up and get it. Order me another brandy."

"Why don't we both go upstairs?" he suggested. "We can read the script in my hotel room. It'll be more comfortable."

She tossed back the remainder of her drink and set the empty glass down solidly on the bar. "That sounds fine, but let's stick to *my* room."

He downed the last of his drink and placed his empty glass beside hers. "We're better off in mine," he advised, getting up off his stool. "My room has a full bar."

The surprise on her face was delicious, but it was nothing compared to the stupefied look in her eyes when he flung open the door to his suite. She remained rooted to the spot, mumbling, "Dominic, it's enormous!"

He said modestly, "I can't complain."

She gave him a quizzical look. His expressionless face told her little.

"Ladies first," he said, waving her into the room.

Her eyes roamed the great walls, taking in the many lavish paintings and the grandiose carvings while he closed the door. She stopped in the center of the room, and her gaze traveled upward to the ornamental ceiling. She noticed the chandelier and let out a tiny gasp.

"Pretty, isn't it?" he said, enjoying her reaction, forgetting that he had reacted precisely the same way earlier in the day.

Once more, she stared at him in wonder, and then the regal canopy bed in the background caught her attention. "My God! Look at that!" she exclaimed, peering over his shoulder.

He looked around anxiously, wondering if there was an intruder. "Oh, the bed, you mean," he said, greatly relieved. "Looks monstrous, doesn't it? Like something from a period drama. Oddly enough, it's surprisingly comfortable."

"Is this really your room, Dominic?"

"Of course. I let you in, didn't I?"

She was giving him a hard look, deeply suspicious of him.

"Christ," he muttered, mildly affronted. "It's not like I'm room-sitting while the real occupant is out having supper."

"But Dominic," she persisted, "how did you get such a lovely room? This isn't some Hollywood movie."

He preferred to fib than tell her that the receptionist had taken a fancy to him and given him a temporary upgrade. It was much more fun to make her think that his stature as an actor had demanded that he be given a luxury suite. "Who knows, and frankly, who cares. As the saying goes, ours is not to reason why, et cetera." He had, in fact, forgotten the rest of the saying.

"I can't believe you have this expensive room," she muttered, pouting.

"If I didn't know better, I'd say there's a reek of resentment in the air," he said derisively. "Your room wouldn't happen to be much smaller than mine, would it?"

She looked chagrined. "Perhaps."

"How much smaller? Half the size?"

"No," she glowered, "it's not even a quarter of the size. In fact, it's probably no bigger than your bathroom."

His lips twisted into a cruel sneer. "Would you like to see the bathroom? It's somewhere around here." He pointed vaguely to the other end of the room, where a curved, narrow corridor separated the bedroom and the bathroom.

"Damn you! I hate this situation," she told him petulantly. "My room should be just as nice as yours. Am I not just as important as you?"

"More important, perhaps. You satisfy Ignacio in ways I never could."

She bristled at the comment. "What the hell does *that* mean?"

He gave a dismissive wave of the hand. "Let's not bicker about trivial things."

The look in her eyes told him she was in the mood for a full-on argument. The size of his room made her wonder about the salary gap between them. Ignacio wasn't the sort to discuss money matters with her, but if this room was any indication of the value he placed on his lead actors, by comparison, she was clearly unappreciated.

"I've been cooped up in airplanes for seventeen hours. I'm owed a good bed for the night. And hey presto! Look what I got for my troubles. Evidently, somebody took pity on me. They knew what I'd endured and wanted me to reside in surroundings befitting my station." With a mischievous smile, Dominic added, "Possibly the person who booked me into the room enjoyed the film *Bolivian Hound*."

Sofía cocked an eyebrow. "That can't possibly be the case."

He laughed merrily. Sofía's crabby attitude didn't bother him in the least. "Why don't you make yourself comfortable while I get us some drinks," he suggested, gesturing toward the bed.

Her irritation was still evident. "I'm not sure if I want to stay in this room. I feel angry just being here."

He nodded sympathetically. "You deserve this, too. You're the main actress, after all. I'm sure Ignacio will fix things tomorrow. In the meantime, let's drink and enjoy the room together."

"I suppose," she said unenthusiastically.

He walked across the room to the bar. "What would you like to drink?"

She sat down on the edge of the bed. "Whiskey."

He rummaged around and found a bottle of bourbon. He examined it approvingly and grabbed two glasses. When he finished pouring the drinks, he noticed she had taken off her shoes and was on his bed, her head resting on his pillow.

He considered her silently, impressed by her silhouette. "Comfy, isn't it?" he remarked as he approached her.

"Uh-huh," she said, not bothering to raise her head. "I don't want to move."

"Then don't."

Reluctantly, she pushed herself into a sitting position. "I have to if I want to enjoy my drink."

He handed her the glass, put his drink on the bedside table, and then headed across the room to his suitcase. He unzipped the front pocket and pulled out a dog-eared movie script.

"You'll have to excuse my notes," he told her, returning to the bed. "I've written all over the script in red ink."

"As long as my lines are legible, it doesn't matter."

She took the script from him and flipped through the pages while he removed his shoes and clambered onto the bed.

"How did you get involved in this picture?" he asked. "Were you also in some ghastly B-movie that Ignacio happened to watch and think you'd be perfect for the role of María?"

She shook her head. "I have known Ignacio for years, ever since acting school. I auditioned for a small part in a television show and got the job. We got on so well that we kept in touch.

Since that show, he has directed me in two television commercials and a music video."

"Is he easy to work for?"

"What do you want me to say? No, he is awful…a monster?"

"If that's the truth, then yes."

"Well, that's not so. He's a wonderful director. An actor's director." Her eyes betrayed her. She could hardly look him in the eye, and the words slinked out her mouth with flagrant dishonesty.

"What should I know about him?" he demanded.

She shrugged her slender shoulders vaguely. "At times, he can seem rather meticulous," she was willing to reveal. "It's almost as if the movie is playing in his head, and he's trying to recreate on celluloid what is taking place in his mind."

"I think I know what that means. Should I expect lots of retakes?"

"You could say that," she said with veiled frankness.

He picked up his drink and took a long, gluttonous sip.

"Are you ready to rehearse?" she asked.

He replaced the glass on the table, mumbling, "As ready as I'll ever be."

He prepared to commit the script to memory, hoping he wouldn't come to hate their scenes. Just how painstaking the shoot would be and how fastidious the director truly was, he had yet to determine.

The unpleasant feeling in the pit of his stomach suggested that he was about to enter Hell.

Six

ONCE more, the howl of the telephone on the bedside table brought Dominic out of his deep sleep. His bloodshot eyes snapped open. He hadn't drawn the curtain last night; sunlight spilled through the large window. He lunged for the telephone, nearly knocking it off the table as he tried to grab the receiver.

"Hello?" His splintered voice sounded grisly, and he became anxious that he had damaged his vocal cords during the night.

"Why are you still in your hotel room, Mister Graves? What has happened?"

He rubbed his eyes, trying to massage away the pain behind them. "Who *is* this?"

"Maria Romero," she announced crossly.

Dominic tried to recall the name, but nothing came to mind. He took the phone away from his ear and took a few deep breaths. There was a severe pounding in his head. The shrill voice emanating from the receiver didn't help.

"Can you repeat that?" he asked, placing the receiver against his ear.

"Romero." She practically screamed the name at him. "I'm Ignacio's personal assistant."

"Of course. Good morning."

"Is there a problem? Are you sick?"

"No. I'm fine," he said, although the hammering in his head declared otherwise. "What time is it?"

"It is eight o'clock. *Eight o'clock*," she repeated with sharp emphasis, intensifying the throbbing sensation in his head. "Everyone is gathered on the set. We are waiting for you!"

He felt an icy chill down his back. "I'll be there shortly."

"You'll be here *at once*!" she commanded.

"I'm leaving right now," he told her, without knowing where he was supposed to be or how he would get there. He also didn't think he was in any condition to go to work.

"A taxi is waiting outside. Don't worry about what clothes to wear or your personal appearance. We will send you to hair and makeup when you arrive."

He put a hand through his hair fretfully. His hair was on end, giving the impression he had slept hanging upside down.

"Also, we can't locate Sofía Prodova. The hotel staff told us she was not in her room. They can't find her anywhere."

He cupped a hand over the receiver and shouted an expletive.

"Tell her to get in the taxi if you see her."

He removed his hand from the mouthpiece and penitently said, "I'll let her know. Thank you. Chau."

He noticed rapid movement beneath the sheets as he put the receiver back in the cradle. It was as if someone were fighting their way out of a sack. Next, he heard a muffled growl, and then a head emerged, generating an ugly wheeze that sounded like a drowning person coming up for air. He stared at the tortured creature beside him, leaning away from it. The bedraggled thing let out a hacking cough that made Dominic recoil. They then beat back the sheets until their arms were free and said gruffly, "What time is it?"

He stared at the ruddy-faced woman with smeared eye makeup and spittle on her chin, wondering what the hell had happened during the night. He had no recollection of this old sow whose manly voice intimated they may be a transvestite.

"Jesus! You're looking at me like you don't remember a thing about last night?"

He turned his head to one side, nauseated by her rancid breath. "I'm sure it will come to me later. Right now, though, I'm having trouble remembering where I am, let alone who I'm with."

She beat her fist against his chest, causing a new pain to register in him. "I ought to scratch my name into your flesh so you don't forget it."

"Or you might simply tell it to me. An introduction would be nice."

Sofía hit him again, even harder this time. As painful as it was, he was thankful she hadn't used her claws on him.

"You're loathsome," she declared. "It's not enough that you take advantage of me. You're determined to ruin my career as well."

She threw back the sheets and climbed out of bed. As she stomped about the room, her body bristled with anger.

He dispassionately examined her naked, willowy figure. There was a lotus flower tattoo on the upper portion of her back, and though he wasn't averse to body tattoos, he didn't typically find them all that interesting. Ones on the neck and face seemed crude and unflattering, while ones on the shoulders and lower back seemed basic and unremarkable. Aware that black and gray tattoos likely originated in prisons in the 1970s and 80s, the snob in him still regarded the style as jailhouse art. However, the strong black tones and the subtle blends of shading revealed the artist's high level of skill and care. The pulsation in his head subsided while he gazed at it.

She bent down, gathered her clothes off the floor, and tossed them on the bed. "Please tell me it isn't six o'clock yet," she said, looking harassed.

"It's much later than that."

"How late?"

"It's eight o'clock."

She sorted through the bundle of clothes with a tortured

expression. Her undeveloped career felt about as tangled and disordered as her garments.

"Didn't you arrange for an alarm call for five-thirty?"

He didn't like the indictment in her voice. "We both slept through it."

She let out an exasperated growl. "If I'm fired because of this, I'll kill you!"

"Yes, darling."

She glared at him as she began to dress. The likelihood of her hitting him on the chest again, harder than before, seemed high.

He gave a cursory glance at her petite body as she put on her padded bra. He thought how substandard her chest looked compared to most of his conquests and wondered why Sofía's attractive, svelte body failed to excite him. Her long, thin limbs and smooth, pale skin had universal appeal. She looked like the sort of striking beauty you find walking down a catwalk, modeling high-end clothes. Yet, without clothes or makeup and in the clear light of day, she was a disappointment. He watched her pull on a pair of G-string panties, idly observing the small, neat strip of hair. It was all very precise and orderly and carefully contrived, just like everything else about her. She didn't seem like the type of woman to let the hair grow on her legs, or be seen in public without makeup, or wear the same pair of underwear two days in a row.

"Must you keep staring at me?" Sofía complained.

With a lethargic sigh, he got out of bed and clambered into his clothes. He didn't hurry, as it hurt his head, and by the time he had finished dressing, she was waiting at the door.

"*What's taking you so long?*" she screamed at him.

"I feel like I'm going to throw up," he admitted.

"If you can't handle your whiskey, you shouldn't drink it."

"I can handle my whiskey just fine," he grumbled. "It didn't mix well with the brandy, that's all."

"I drank brandy as well, and I feel fine."

"But did you also have wine in the afternoon?"

"Yes," she said frankly.

He gave her a disgruntled look, hissing, "Aren't you just a peach. Your mother must be so goddamn proud. Is she also a lush?"

Her fiery eyes signaled that he had just dug his own grave with that remark, and she scampered across the room, seized by an impulse to mangle his pretty-boy face. She snatched a sturdy ashtray off the coffee table as she ran and struck him in the chest with it. As he doubled over, gasping for air, she brought the ashtray down hard on his back, between his shoulder blades. He went down on one knee, a winded mess, struggling to draw breath but striving to beg for mercy. The ashtray caught him again, glancing off his shoulder, nearly putting him face-down on the carpet, sending shockwaves through him. He was about to be wiped out by his costar in a most barbaric way. He hadn't even made it onto the set!

He mumbled inarticulately about the need to get something on celluloid—a first scene in the can—but she didn't hear him. She raised the ashtray once more, determined to strike again, and it suddenly dawned on him that he didn't even smoke. He hated the smell of tobacco and felt nauseous at the taste of it on a woman's tongue.

She brought the ashtray down again, clonking him on the head with it, knocking him to the ground. As she glowered at him, sprawled out across the floor, unmoving, her attitude quickly changed. The anger turned to horror, and panic swept over her. Then the ashtray dropped from her fingers, hitting the carpet with an ugly thump and rolling to one side. She put her hands over her mouth to stifle a scream.

Seven

THE world began to swirl. Sofía Prodova's swish, privileged existence was on the verge of becoming a nightmare.

What the hell have I done? she fretted. *This isn't me. This can't have happened.*

The sight of Dominic's comatose form, unnaturally spread-eagled, made her lightheaded. *I've killed him! Beaten him to death!*

The impulse to punish him for his malevolent tongue had backfired horribly. This was destructive, not correctional. *I've ruined everything*, she realized, sickened by the extent of her vicious anger.

She poked him with her foot, and when that did nothing, she fell to her knees, and her hands went to his face, slapping his cheeks softly, at first, and then harder when he didn't respond.

"Wake up! Wake up!"

Carelessly, she began beating him in the face with cold, hard malice, growling at him to awaken, but no matter how much she shook him and spanked his rubbery skin, she couldn't seem to revive him. *The medics might not, either*, she thought, shivering all over.

His body was limp in her arms, lifeless. A rising talent fading fast—at her hands.

"Goddammit!" she screamed.

She tried to wrestle him into a sitting position but managed only to turn him over onto his back. His pallid face was not a welcome sight. The loveliness was gone from it, the wondrousness of life snatched away.

"You utter bastard! You pathetic, nauseating weakling!" She scowled at him hatefully, hissing venomously, "Come back to life. Wake up, you son of a bitch!"

She wanted him alive—if only so she could kill him properly.

He didn't blink, didn't stir. Like before, during their lovemaking, he didn't give her what she desired.

She pressed her forehead against his sorrowfully. She wouldn't mourn Dominic's passing—she was sure nobody would pine the death of this ill-mannered plaything. She was, in fact, grieving over her short-lived career.

"This might have been the start of something wonderful," she sobbed, thinking of the unmade movie. "I hate you. I hate you. I hate you."

She said it over and over, willing his eyes to open. Then she gently rested his head on the carpet and checked his neck and wrist for a pulse, hoping for a miracle. There was no indication that he was breathing, no signs of life that she could detect. Disaster had struck—mercilessly, savagely—and she was the culprit.

It was time to seek help. Time to volunteer a testimony and begin the deceit.

She ran to the telephone to call the front desk. It was imperative that she absolved herself from any wrongdoing and established that this calamity was nothing but an accident. "The actor fell and struck his head," she said aloud to nobody. She tried that statement again with more sincerity, but something about it didn't ring true.

She left the telephone receiver in the cradle and rushed back across the room, stepping over the body with care. The ashtray was on her mind. The instrument of death. The evidence.

She retrieved it and shoved it in her pocket, intending to discard it later, somewhere that it would never be found.

As she hurried back to the telephone, she caught her foot

on Dominic's flaccid body and fell clumsily. She landed heavily beside him, squealing as she hit the deck. Though it seemed like an impressively rough tumble, somehow, she managed not to hurt herself.

She peered at him crossly, thinking: *He's still proving to be a nuisance.*

Then the miracle happened, the phenomenon that instantly changed her life once more. Unexpectedly—pleasingly—the actor began to stir.

"Oh my God!" she gasped with delight. "You're alive! Oh, thank God!"

He groaned and rolled onto his side, muttering, "What the hell happened?"

She touched his cheek, caressing him tenderly, delighted he had uttered a coherent sentence. With joy in her voice, she murmured, "You fell and struck your head. Are you okay, dear?"

With some effort, he pulled himself into a sitting position. His hand went to the back of his head. "I swear my head is about to explode."

"It's the hangover," she insisted. "You drink too much."

He shook his head and immediately regretted it. "I hang out with the wrong people."

"Can you walk?"

"My head will fall off if I try to get up."

"I'll get you some water."

"I need painkillers."

She was in total agreement. Fearing he may have a concussion, she brought him Tylenol rather than aspirin and gave him a visual test. Minutes later, she made him close his eyes and stand with his feet together, then with one foot in front of the other, and then on one leg.

"Do you know where you are?" she asked him as he performed the tests. "Do you know why you're here?"

"Apparently, I'm the unlucky bastard who has to endure your

games. What are you going to make me do next? A handstand?"

"You don't have a concussion," she said irritably. "Just women issues."

"Ain't that the truth," he agreed with a despairing sigh.

"C'mon, let's go," she ordered.

He assumed they were headed for the hospital, but that was the last thing on Sofía's mind. As he was up and breathing, capable of walking and talking and making glib comments, she was determined to get them both to the movie set.

She grabbed his arm and escorted him to the door.

"Not so quickly," he begged. "My head can't take it."

"You can idle later. Right now, we're wanted on the set."

"Oh, man," he whimpered. "I'm in no fit state to act."

"Pull yourself together," she scolded, giving him a shove in the back.

When they exited the room, she hurriedly made her way along the corridor, several paces ahead of him.

"It's so damning that we're both arriving late," she muttered while they rode the elevator. "What the hell am I gonna tell Ignacio?"

"The truth for a change," he snidely remarked.

She thrust her hands in her pockets, resisting the temptation to strangle him. The feel of the ashtray reminded her that she couldn't afford another mistake. She needed to keep her temper in check.

"Just keep quiet about last night," she commanded.

"Difficult. Everyone knows full well why we're late."

"You hit your head. I tended to you until you gained consciousness. That's what we'll say."

"I fell, is that right?"

Her earnest nod impressed him.

"Unfortunately, the lie won't scotch the rumors."

"Rumors? What rumors?"

"Everyone is aware of your sexual impropriety."

"My *what?*" she responded, affronted.

"Ignacio's personal assistant…I forget her name…"

"Maria Romero."

"She told me that none of the hotel staff could find you this morning. They know you weren't in your room. You weren't to be found anywhere."

Sofía was disturbed by the news. "She said that?"

"Yes. And it doesn't take a detective to guess where you were," he said with enjoyment.

Her fingers gripped the ashtray fiercely. The desire to clobber him with it again was extraordinarily intense. How he was able to arouse in her such maddening feelings of frustration and loathing was incredible.

She glowered at him, thinking: *Someone, someday, is going to throttle the life out of Dominic Graves.*

She prayed someone would beat her to it.

Eight

AS Dominic approached the director, he stumbled over a folding chair and avoided toppling headfirst into Ignacio's lap by placing his hands firmly against the director's thighs.

"*Idiota torpe!*" growled Ignacio. "Watch where you put your hands!"

Dominic muttered a few silent oaths and inelegantly detached himself from the director. Pinning the blame firmly on the chair, he lashed out at it with unexpected savagery. His foot ripped through the canvas, and the chair leaped into the air.

The actress let out a voluble shriek. It was the stomach-churning kind that could placate the demands of the most finicky horror movie fan.

The chair narrowly missed her head and clattered to the ground two feet away.

Ignacio stared cagily at Dominic, unsure if his lead actor had genuinely gone berserk or was giving him a demonstration of his acting prowess.

Dominic instantly regained his composure and apologized profusely for his behavior.

"You're a crazy fool," hissed Sofía, finding his reckless outburst juvenile and unpardonable.

She viciously elbowed him out of her way, wishing she could hit him between the legs instead. The way he had almost decapitated her with a chair made her wonder what other mischief he was capable of and how many bruises she would end up with during their love scenes.

"Ignacio, forgive me. I..."

"Enough!" snapped Ignacio. There was the same savage look in his eyes that his lead actor had exhibited a moment earlier while vandalizing the canvass chair. "Oh, for Christ's sake, do something useful, woman. Pick up that chair!"

His unnaturally aggressive behavior startled her. The sweet affection bestowed on her over the years seemed to have evaporated entirely.

"Ignacio, darling," she began, taking a step closer. "Don't treat me this way...."

The syrupy tone in her voice didn't soften his mood. "I said pick that damn chair up!"

Dominic swiftly assessed the dark look on Ignacio's face and decided to intervene, anticipating the quarrel would escalate. "Cut! Let's start over. Try it with cheerful faces this time." He put his arms together, making them into a clapperboard, and said, "Scene one, take two."

"Enough!" shouted Ignacio, rising to his feet. "Do you have any idea what time it is?"

Dominic automatically glanced at his wrist, then realized that in his haste, he had left his watch on the dresser.

"It's after eight o'clock," said Ignacio angrily. "You were supposed to be here at six o'clock sharp. Didn't I make that clear last night?"

"Ah, yes, about that...."

"What must I do to get you to turn up when I need you?" The vacant look in Dominic's eyes prompted him to go on. "Maybe a nice bed in a luxury hotel is wrong for you both. Maybe we need to set you up here, on the college grounds, with a simple tent and a sleeping bag."

Dominic's plucky smile quickly faded. "Camping isn't really my thing. Can't sleep a wink."

"Ah, most interesting," responded the director, as though he had found the solution to his problem. "Too much of a good thing can be bad for you. Too much sleep, for example, is a terrible thing. When you sleep all morning and show up here late, that is catastrophic for me."

"The outdoors plays havoc with my allergies," explained Dominic.

Sofía put a hand on his arm to quiet him. "Today was a one-off. Mornings won't be a problem from now on."

"You'll do as you're told, will you?" Ignacio said contemptuously. "Then where is that chair I asked you to pick up?"

His snappish manner wounded Sofía. The evening before, they had acted like old lovers, but now he seemed disgusted by the sight of her. His scolding eyes stalked her with rising bitterness as she retrieved the chair. It wasn't clear if he would look at her again with quite the same affection.

Sensibly, Dominic kept his mouth shut. He wished he had done that the moment he arrived on the set.

Ignacio turned to Dominic. The scowl was no longer on his face. "Roberto Luguano once sat in that chair," he said proudly.

Dominic nodded approvingly, trying to muster some reverence in his expression, though he hadn't the faintest idea who Roberto Luguano was or why it mattered that the man had once sat in the chair.

"One of Uruguay's finest actors," continued Ignacio. "He was known for his comic roles, but I tell you, the man was an even better serious actor. I saw him in a stage play once. A tragedy about a world-famous ventriloquist who loses his voice. He was so marvelous, I wept uncontrollably at the end of the play."

Sofía returned with the chair, opened it, and placed it back in its rightful position. The prized piece of furniture now looked rickety and beyond repair.

"Sit," said Ignacio, urging Dominic into the collapsible seat.

Dominic lowered himself cautiously into it, expecting it to

give way at any second. There was a ripping sound as the tear in the canvass increased. His buttocks sank into the torn gash until he was trapped in the frame, unable to move.

Nobody's face showed signs of amusement.

Ignacio invited Sofía to sit. The coldness in his voice made it sound like an order. She perched on the edge of a folding seat, looking ready to spring out of it at a moment's notice.

"I told you six o'clock because we have to shoot big scenes today, and I want to take advantage of the sunlight," Ignacio explained, unfazed by Dominic's awkward wriggling. "Now we have lost more than two hours."

He sighed and gazed around at the group of men fussing around a stunt police car and a couple of motorbikes, setting up one of the movie's many action scenes. While some had been completed entirely by a second production unit, without the director or crew present, Ignacio was keen to maintain the impression that he was overseeing every frame of the movie. His specialties were straightforward, conventional car chases and gun fights, though he liked to keep the shot footage as raw and under-edited as possible. Noise, pacing, and continuity were key aspects for him. He wanted to hear the dialogue over the top of an explosion and make the audience feel the full impact of two cars colliding. It was important to him that most of what was shot made it into the finished film, with little lost in the editing process. Budgetary constraints and tight production schedules kept him from meddling in the construction of some action sequences, but every moment Dominic was on-screen, Ignacio was duty-bound to be at the helm.

Dominic gave up trying to extract himself from the chair. He crossed his left leg over the right knee and put his hands behind his head, pretending he had found a comfortable position.

"There is so much to do, and the clock is ticking," muttered Ignacio forlornly. Looking back at Dominic, he was appalled by the languid way the actor was sprawled in his seat.

Noticing Ignacio's disgusted expression, Dominic swiftly uncrossed his legs and put his hands down by his side, trying not to look so at ease.

"Maybe we can adjust the shooting schedule and make it work, but it will not be easy. We may have to work through the night. We will do what we can. I hope it's enough."

Dominic's headache grew stronger. He wondered if somebody had a packet of aspirin on hand.

"Don't ever let this happen again," Ignacio warned, glowering at them both. "We have this beautiful college campus to ourselves for only two days. We must make full use of it. We need all the daylight hours we can get."

The rustle of paper and clomping feet caught his attention, and he turned around to look at the gangly figure of the cameraman approaching. The lanky man was walking with his head down, absorbedly looking at the various drawings on a poster board. He looked up just in time to avoid walking into a tree.

Ignacio gave a wearied sigh. "Okay, that's all. Daniela and Eliana are waiting for you. They will sort out your hair and costumes."

Sofía attempted to say something, but he waved her away dismissively. "Go. The set is nearly ready. I will call you when I need you. And don't be late this time," he warned.

He stood and moved toward the cameraman, turning his back on Dominic and Sofía.

"Well, that didn't go so well," remarked Dominic, scratching the back of his neck. "On the bright side, at least he didn't fire me."

Sofía's hateful stare disheartened him.

Fortuitously, Maria Romero appeared behind them just as Sofía was about to rebuke him. He turned around, pleased to escape Sofía's reproachful stare, but his face dropped at the sight of the moody, heavyset woman.

"Dominic, you've shown up at last," she said icily.

"It's nice to meet you, Mary," he fibbed, holding out his hand.

"Maria," she snapped, clasping his hand and giving it a rough jiggle. "If you can't remember my name, how will you ever remember your lines?"

It was a fair question, but he hated her asking it. She was young, blunt, and not bothered about denting a man's ego. Didn't she know that an actor was the most fragile man of all? Pull at a thread, and the ego might unravel completely.

"I prefer words on a page to faces. Anyway, I wish you'd phoned me earlier this morning," he complained, "before eight-thirty. It might have saved me much embarrassment."

"I telephoned you at six thirty this morning," she flatly informed him. "And again at seven o'clock…and seven thirty… and…"

"Is that so?" he said awkwardly. "I must be a heavy sleeper."

Sofía had a furious look on her face. "I'm going to find Daniela and Eliana."

She barged past Dominic and stormed across the expansive grounds toward the college's main building, which peeped out over a thick line of trees.

"Is she always such a fiery creature?" he said, staring fixedly at Sofía as she marched into the distance.

"She's usually worse than that. She acts like a spoiled child, and nobody dares stand up to her."

This time, Maria's candor pleased him. He wished she would always save disparaging remarks for someone other than him.

"All except Ignacio," he muttered, half to himself. "Those two seem to be cast in the same mold." When Sofía was so far away he could no longer appreciate her delicately sculpted figure, he turned to face Maria, saying openly, "I made a bad impression on Ignacio today. He's in a tetchy mood. You know him well?"

"I've worked for him for the last eight months."

"That long, huh? He seemed about ready to wring my neck."

"I'm sure he can't be the only one."

He ignored the jibe. "Will he calm down by this afternoon? Or will I be getting my ass kicked all day?"

She shrugged. "His mood changes with the wind. However, when he's in a bad mood, he has been known to get very mad."

"Uh-huh. How mad?"

"Once, during lunch with some of the actors and crew, he got so angry he stabbed one of the background actors in the leg with a fork."

Dominic thought back to his dinner with Ignacio the previous night. The man had seemed abnormally passionate about his food. "What were they arguing over, the dessert tray?"

"Sofía."

A flicker of concern passed across Dominic's face. "What about her?"

"I don't know all the details. Ignacio and Sofía have strong feelings for each other. I'm sure you know this already."

Dominic said nothing. Though he suspected some sexual bond existed between them, he assumed they liked to keep things casual. The way Sofía had jumped into bed with him, he figured she was unattached and wholly available.

"As I understand it, the actor saw more of Sofía than he had a right to."

"Hm. That so?"

"Ignacio became upset about the romance. Something was said during lunch. Whatever it was, it sent Ignacio into a rage, and he sank his fork into the man's leg. The medic removed it and stitched up the man's wound."

Dominic gave an involuntary shudder. "This happened recently?"

"It happened last week. It caused quite a commotion." A grim smirk played on her lips. "Now everybody knows not to mess around with Sofía."

Dominic smiled tightly. "Well, that's good to know."

Maria removed a leaf of paper from the slim leather file

held against her chest. "Here's the schedule for today," she said, handing him the daily call sheet.

He took it without much interest, rolled it up, and shoved it in his pocket. "Is there any chance I can get a couple of aspirin?"

"You have a bad head?"

"A wicked one. It feels like a rodent has burrowed into my skull and is gnawing at my eye sockets."

She looked amused rather than concerned. "Go to Daniela so she can get you ready for your scenes. I'll tell her to put aspirin and a bottle of water aside for you."

He nodded and started to walk away, but she stopped him. "Go across the grass," she advised, pointing him in a different direction. "It is a shortcut to the main building."

He made his way sluggishly across the soft grass, passing between many varieties of tall trees. He glimpsed several striking buildings in the distance and thought how nice-looking the private college was and how refreshing it was to have a naturally scenic backdrop. According to the film script, much of the action occurred in police stations, beauty parlors, and slum areas. With its peaceful and picturesque grounds, the college seemed an unlikely setting for a violent, all-action crime story.

He tried to ignore that violence, bloodshed, and infamy could unfold anywhere.

After staggering up a hilly section of ground, feeling like he was getting quite the workout, he paused at the top for a breather. Ahead of him were hordes of students employed as extras on the film. The lush, wooded gardens behind him were in stark contrast to the noisy bustle of people milling around the main campus. A frail, rather elderly woman grabbed his wrist as he passed by the large crowd.

"At last. Come," she said in a shrewish voice. "I'm waiting forever."

"I take it you must be Daniela?"

"This way. Hurry."

He followed her into the building, noticing that the signage and the façade had been altered slightly to give it the appearance of a traditional college. They passed through a broad corridor, sunlight pouring through the high glass ceiling. Halfway along the passageway, she led him into a large room with a gleaming reception desk, the shelves behind it lined with an extensive selection of hair products. He glanced around the room at the rows of long mirrors and washbasins. Half a dozen women were sitting on red-colored swivel chairs in front of the mirrors.

"This is quite the setup you have here. Looks like a real salon."

"It is."

"The college has a hair salon?"

"Yes. They teach beauty therapy here," she said, signaling for him to sit. "That's why we're filming here and not in town. The scenes where Bruce first meets María will be shot in this salon."

She grabbed a lightweight, black hairdresser's gown off the hook and put it around him, fastening it at his neck.

"Just a short back and sides today, dear," he told her.

She was unmoved by his jocular remark. "Your hair must be cut just so, exactly as Ignacio has instructed. I'll trim the front but leave the sides and back long. And I'll give you a side part here," she said, drawing a line along his scalp with her finger.

"Is that how the newspaper journalists over here wear their hair? Seems a bit dreary."

"It's the look Ignacio wants for you."

"Guess I should be thankful he doesn't want my hair thin on top and with a bald patch at the crown."

"Yes," she agreed, fingering his hair. "You have nice, thick hair. It is good we keep it that way."

She sprayed his hair liberally with water and put a comb through it with rather brutish force. Eventually, she picked up the scissors and started to cut. He glanced at the mirror before him and saw Sofía seated at a workstation behind him. She watched him raptly in her mirror while her own hair was styled. He gave her a roguish wink.

"Maria telephoned me five minutes ago," said Daniela, concentrating on the back of his head. "She told me you have a hangover."

"Did she now?" he said, displeased. "I told her I had a headache."

"A headache from alcohol? I can smell it on you. Very potent. You want something to make it go away?"

"Yes, please. Aspirin if you've got it."

"You want beer?"

"Beer for breakfast!" Dominic crumpled his face. "What are you saying? That I'm an alcoholic?"

Daniela's expressionless eyes studied him in the mirror. "You don't want beer?"

Dominic sucked on a tooth for a moment, then he shrugged and said, "Sure."

She stopped cutting his hair and walked across the room to a discreet refrigerator behind the reception desk. When she returned, she was carrying two bottles of Cerveza Patricia and a bottle opener. She pried the top off both bottles and handed him one.

He thanked her. It wasn't often he started the day with liquor, but hair of the dog might be just what he needed. He took a lengthy swig and let out a satisfied sigh. "Now that's good breakfast."

He turned the bottle in his palm, memorizing the label. While Daniela continued to cut his hair, he gazed into the mirror, happy to see some color back in his cheeks. Having endured a monstrous ache in his head all morning, he was finally experiencing something nearing relief.

He then became aware of the apprehension in Sofía's stare. She was watching him closely, grinding her teeth.

He couldn't blame her. She had every right to be concerned. The last thing any actor wants to see is their co-star boozing it up shortly before their first scene.

He sighed and took another long draw on his beer. *To hell with decorum and self-restraint.*

Daniela gripped him by the crown and repositioned his head. "Keep still," she insisted.

She ran her scissors through his hair, snipping very lightly and speedily. The haircut didn't take long, and when she was done, he noticed there weren't a lot of hair clippings on his gown or the floor. She started the water running in the sink. "Put your head back."

He nodded but finished his beer first.

She was rough with her fingers once his head was in the washbasin. He could feel her nails digging into his scalp as she applied shampoo. With his eyes tightly shut, he imagined he was charging through dense woodland, the branches of a tree scratching against his head. Just like the haircut, the hair wash was over quickly. The water felt cold as she sprayed it over his head. It felt so unpleasant that he didn't care if she washed out all the shampoo.

"All done," she informed him, lifting his head out of the basin.

She threw a coarse towel over his head and vigorously dried the hair until his scalp felt tender. He looked in the mirror, half expecting to see a bald patch where the towel had chafed.

"Wait," she said, sensing he was about to flee. "I need to style it."

As she searched her workstation for a hairbrush, he leaned over and picked up the other beer bottle, feeling he had earned it.

Sofía stopped behind him and said, "How many of those are you going to drink? It's not nine o'clock yet."

"Must you nag? You're beginning to sound like my mother."

"You should have listened to her more," she said huffily. "My mother is dead. And she wasn't a lush!"

It was a relief when she stormed out of the salon.

Way to go, Dom, he thought dolefully. *You sure know how to get a woman all hot and bothered. That cruel, ill-chosen putdown nearly goaded a woman into putting you down…permanently.*

The scary situation reminded him that his harsh tongue was a powerful weapon that could cause all sorts of harm. And it could incite the kind of senseless chaos that wrecked lives.

He took another long swig of his beer, soaking his rough tongue in the liquid. As a temporary measure, it worked better than two aspirin, subduing his headache and buoying his spirits.

All too quickly, he emptied the bottle, glugging down the fluid like water. Then he waggled the empty bottle at Daniela. "I'll have another when you get a moment," he insisted, planning to slay that headache the best way he knew how.

Nine

HE staggered out of the building and into the sunlight, looking ghastly yet feeling on top of the world. Eliana had taken a long time on his makeup—far longer than she had spent on Sofía's face. The scene they were about to shoot required Dominic to sport a black eye and swollen lip. His character also had a faded scar just above his temple.

As he sauntered across the grounds, drawing the attention of many extras, he knew Eliana had done an excellent job of making him look like he had been on the losing end of a street fight.

Sebastián Pereira, the assistant director, roared harshly at the people around him frantically getting things ready for the scene. He raised his voice above the babbling voices, dropping the f-bomb with increasing frequency. He sounded like a drill sergeant, and when he noticed Dominic, he glanced at his watch, barking, "You're late. Should have been here an hour ago. We're almost ready to shoot."

Sebastián moved away, continuing to boss the crew about with mean satisfaction. He dearly wished his cantankerous words would cause greater impact. If one person threw down their equipment in a fit of temper, he would feel like he had succeeded, that he had finally earned the respect of his faux platoon. Alas, the louder his voice, the smaller he appeared to them. Indeed, many had already tuned him out completely. A niggling feeling in the pit of his stomach told him Dominic would soon do the same.

As for Dominic, he could tell already that Sebastián was a rude and pompous prig. Here was a man who was tolerated rather than liked, who snarled and barked but wasn't feared. Watching the crew filter past him like he wasn't there made Dominic keen to follow suit. Accordingly, he gave Sebastián a wide berth but didn't stray too far from the production crew.

After nearly half an hour, Ignacio quietly emerged, somehow unseen. He dropped his powerful hand on Dominic's shoulder, surprising the actor.

Dominic's startled yell amused him. "My God," he said, grinning. "You're as jumpy as a grasshopper."

When Dominic turned around, it was Ignacio's turn to gasp. "Jeez. You look ghastly. The makeup is terrific."

Dominic's heart was still racing. He took a moment to catch his breath and then said evenly, "I hardly recognized myself in the mirror."

A tiny frown appeared on Ignacio's shiny forehead. He leaned in close to Dominic, sniffing deeply. "Have you been drinking?"

The stern gleam in his eye communicated that he didn't abide actors imbibing before a scene.

"No, no," Dominic insisted, inching away from him. "I make it a rule never to touch alcohol before noon."

Ignacio's eyes narrowed. "I smell alcohol on your breath."

"Must be from last night. I didn't have a chance to brush my teeth this morning."

"That smell is very potent," said Ignacio, looking skeptically at Dominic. "Exactly how much did you drink last night?"

"Okay, everybody into position," hollered Sebastián.

Ignacio glanced distractedly at the man. When he turned back to Dominic, he seemed to have forgotten the matter entirely. "I want to convey a sense of danger. You and Luis are gutsy men who fear nothing, not even a bullet to the gut. You are both savage men. When placed in a hazardous situation, anything can happen. This is when the two characters come face-to-face for the last time. Remember, there is deep hatred between these two men. Any little thing might set them off."

Ignacio stole a quick peek at Luis, standing a few meters away. The swarthy-looking man adjusted the police cap on his head, exposing the sheen of sweat on his forehead. His black, bushy eyebrows and the several days' growth on his face gave him a dark, menacing edge. He was watching Ignacio intently, bobbing his head thoughtfully from time to time.

"When Luis grabs you by the collar, that's the spark that ignites your fury. You wrestle and exchange blows. Luis knocks you to the ground, but you get up. When you lunge at him, I want you to go for his gun," said Ignacio insistently. "Your character wants to use the gun to get him to talk. You want him to tell you everything."

Dominic frowned. "You want me to get his gun?"

"You won't be able to; Luis will stop you. But I want the struggle to look authentic. No stuntmen, the camera in close, and both of you competing for dominance. Go into the scene with the idea that you *will* get his gun, no matter how often he knocks you down." He took his position beside the assistant director. "Okay, everybody in position."

When he gave the signal, Luis seized Dominic aggressively by the collar. Dominic reached for the man's firearm, getting his fingers to the butt, but before he could yank it from the holster, Luis elbowed him in the ribs and swung a fist at him. The punch glanced off Dominic's cheek, knocking him to the ground.

"Perfect!" Ignacio roared, looking delighted.

Dominic turned on his side and heaved.

"*Maldito!*" grumbled Sebastián, seeing vomit splatter over the grass.

"Are you okay, Dominic?" asked the shocked director. "Should we send for the medic?"

Dominic sat up, massaging his cheekbone. "I'm okay. There's no need for a medic." If anything, he felt slightly better for having thrown up. "I guess that'll teach me a lesson for having a liquid breakfast."

"I knew it!" said Ignacio crossly.

He regretted ordering wine during their meal at the hotel restaurant. He hated working with actors who had drinking problems, and suggesting a nightcap at the bar was a further mistake. Clearly, Dominic could not drink responsibly. Ignacio gazed at his actor with genuine concern. He wanted to fire him.

"Do you need time to recover?" asked Sebastián Pereira.

Dominic pulled his knees up and hunched over them. He took a deep breath and wiped his mouth with the back of his hand. "Yes. Give me a minute, please."

The assistant director glanced anxiously at his watch, muttering to himself.

The blow to Dominic's face was minor, and the discomfort was fleeting, but the taste of vomit lingered.

"Incidentally, I thought that scene was good, Dominic," said Ignacio. "Think you can do it again, exactly the same?"

The actor got to his feet sluggishly and dusted himself down. That punch had come awfully close to dislodging some teeth. He gave his fellow actor a wary look. Pure luck had kept Luis' knuckles from doing more than merely grazing his face.

"Okay," said Ignacio, sensing Dominic was ready. "Let's go for a take."

Sebastián jumped into action, yelling, "Quiet everyone!"

Dominic shuffled to his mark, and the other man moved back into position. Dominic stared at him tensely, waiting while the cinematographer instructed the cameraman to take a medium shot.

"Roll it," Sebastián instructed.

Dominic heard several other voices in sequence.

"Rolling."

"Speed."

"Twenty-three, take one."

A clapperboard was held up in front of his face. Moments later, it snapped shut, and Ignacio yelled, "Action!"

Dominic felt the actor's massive hand on his collar, and before he had managed to reach for the gun, Luis jammed a solid fist in his stomach.

"Cut!" Ignacio roared.

Dominic doubled over, wheezing. His stomach was churning, and he thought he might heave again.

"Dominic, your character is supposed to be tough. He must be able to handle a punch. Don't screw your face up when he hits you."

"It's a genuine reaction!" griped Dominic. "Isn't that what you wanted?"

Ignacio took offense at the hostility in the actor's voice. He wasn't used to being shouted at.

"He's not supposed to really hit me!"

"I hardly touched him," protested Luis.

Ignacio's face was full of disapproval. "I want the camera to capture what looks like a bona fide brawl between two tough men. Sometimes, things don't go quite as anticipated. Next time, continue with the scene, for heaven's sake. We'll keep the camera rolling. Don't be afraid to improvise a little."

Dominic shot him a bitter glance. He wasn't good at improvisation. In fact, he hated the word, equating it with directors who hadn't visualized the scene previously.

"Improvisation is better suited to live theater than a film set," he blurted out.

"What's that?" said Ignacio, taken aback.

"Shouldn't it be choreographed? Can't we rehearse the scene beforehand?"

The director stared at him indignantly. He was fighting back his anger but somehow maintaining a placid expression. "Go on."

"I like everything scripted and planned. I like to see a piece of tape on the floor, indicating where to stand. I'm uncomfortable with it this way," he argued, straightening up. "I don't want Luis knocking my teeth out. If that's the deal, let's get my stuntman in here. Let him face the real punches."

Ignacio clenched his fist, looking like he might take a swing at his actor. He gazed around at his crew, taking a deep breath, allowing himself a moment to let his ire sizzle away. Past confrontations had landed him in some tight situations. His inability to handle them appropriately had stalled his career.

He shut his eyes and silently counted to ten, stamping his feet with the numbers, just like his therapist had advised.

"Yes, yes, I understand," he told Dominic, nodding sympathetically.

The transformation in him was astounding. Ignacio marveled at how he had been able to turn off his anger as if powered by an internal switch.

He turned to Luis. "Don't hit him in the stomach again. We wouldn't want him to throw up on you."

With some reluctance and a bold show of dissatisfaction, Dominic slowly got back into position. He was proud of himself for standing up to Ignacio, wishing he had been as assertive on previous projects. He was tired of uncaring directors putting him in danger and allowing him to get battered and bruised during action scenes. Fear of seeming like a prima-donna had kept him silent too long. It was time he stood up for himself and his rights.

When he began the next take, he was brimming with sureness, determined not to let Luis get the better of him. He pounced at his co-star, reaching for the man's holster, but this time, Luis twisted away from him the moment his fingers brushed against the handgun. The firearm leaped out of the leather gun case and fell to the ground.

Dominic pounced on it, then stifled a scream as Luis stepped on his hand with the heel of his boot. Motivated by a desire for retribution, Dominic grabbed the man by the ankle with his free hand and yanked hard, causing the burly actor to fall.

Luis landed solidly on his back, muttering oaths. He was surprised by Dominic's pace—annoyed by it, in fact.

Though rotund and heavy, Luis was a sprightly man. He scrambled to his feet like a WWE superstar wrestler. He spun around in time to see Dominic level the gun at him.

The camera continued to roll, the director reluctant to yell, "Cut." Nobody said a word.

Luis stared at the muzzle of the gun, watching Dominic slowly lower the weapon until it was aimed at his leg. He thought he saw Dominic's finger tighten on the trigger, and his eyes grew wide with alarm. In panic, he swung his foot at Dominic, striking the actor's wrist with his heavy boot.

Dominic's arm was whipped back, the muzzle pointed at the assistant director.

There was a shrill explosion as the gun unexpectedly discharged.

Ten

THE bullet whistled over Sebastián's head.

"Cut!" yelled Ignacio, horrified.

The gun fell from Dominic's hand, dropping harmlessly into the grass. He spun around wildly and stared at the director in confusion. "Jesus! Was that a blank or a real bullet?"

Ignacio ground his teeth. There was a trace of menace in his eyes. "*Idiota*. Have you never handled a gun before?"

"What? Yes. I don't...."

"You might have shut down the production. Never pull the goddamn trigger on a gun unless the director tells you to do it!"

"That was a real bullet, wasn't it?"

"Of course it was a real bullet," Ignacio said in a low voice. "We're using live ammunition."

"Oh my God!" gasped Dominic, feeling faint. "I nearly *killed* someone!"

Ignacio turned to the assistant director, who was visibly shaking. "As scary as that was, I actually liked that take. It was fantastic, wasn't it?"

Sebastián was too shocked to reply.

"But he didn't deliver his lines," continued Ignacio, shaking his head with frustration. "We go again, but please, try to capture it like that take."

"Wait! What? You can't be serious," gulped Sebastián, dismayed. "He nearly blew my head off!"

Ignacio nodded, oblivious to the man's distress. "We do it again. Luis, pick up your gun. Put it back in your holster. This time, wrestle with Dominic longer and let him take your gun, but please make sure he doesn't actually pull the trigger."

The noisy murmurs of dismay were difficult to ignore. All the same, Ignacio seemed oblivious to his crew's objections.

"Okay, we go again," he said to his crew.

The typically sedate Luis scratched his chin contemplatively, quietly commenting, "You don't think we should switch to blanks?"

"No, I do not!" responded Ignacio tetchily. "I think an actor should act, not argue with the director. Put the gun back in your holster. We go again."

"This is insane! I'm not doing the scene," protested Dominic, stubbornly, incensed that the hare-brained director had put everyone's lives at stake. "The assistant director was nearly shot dead."

"There is no injury on the set," said Ignacio crossly. "Nobody is hurt. Nobody is about to die."

Dominic folded his arms and scowled at the director. "When I tell my agent about this, let's see what people say."

"Your agent won't say shit!" roared Ignacio. "And if you want to slander me to the press, let's see what impact it has on your career."

Dominic unfolded his arms and quickly looked around him for support. He planned to make the director pay for those threats.

The director of photography threw up his hands, saying, "I have two young children."

"What of it?" shrugged Ignacio, mystified.

"He might kill us," explained the gawky cameraman, jerking a shaky finger at Dominic. "We have wives and children to support."

The murderous look in Ignacio's eyes made the man regret having said anything. "We wouldn't want you to have any more accidents. How's your arm?"

Fear washed over the man as Ignacio moved toward him, fixated on his arm.

"It's healing well," he said, backing away.

Ignacio made a determined grab at the man's elbow, muttering, "Let's have a look."

The cameraman twisted away from him, but the rapid movement sent an agonizing spasm through his fragile arm. He winced, clutching his forearm.

"Still tender, I see," remarked Ignacio, sneering meanly. "Perhaps you should consider taking some time away from the picture to allow it to recover fully."

"I can hold the camera just fine," he protested through clenched teeth.

"Then get back behind the camera," advised Ignacio impatiently. "If you don't want to do this scene my way, you can leave the set now."

Dominic saw the cameraman retreating and assumed he was vacating the set. He anticipated others to do likewise.

"You can't threaten us," he said defiantly, figuring that Ignacio would have to back down or there would be a mass exodus. "We won't do the scene, and you'll never live this moment down."

"For some of you, this might be the right moment to think about a career change," said Ignacio, addressing his entire crew. "Anyone wanting to walk off my picture sure as hell won't be working on a film set again."

"You don't really expect people to stay?" said Dominic, frowning.

"I do," replied Ignacio confidently. He cast a baleful glance at the cameraman, growling, "Especially those with wives and young children to support."

"Well, you can't make this picture without the lead star," Dominic brazenly told him. "If live ammo stays, then this actor exits."

"Is that so?" Ignacio muttered broodingly. "Let me put it this way, Dominic. If you don't get back into position…if you stall this movie any longer…I'll phone that agent of yours and tell him exactly what you've just said. Bernie Finkelman—that's his name, isn't it?"

"That's right," nodded Dominic, slightly disquieted by the mention of his agent's name.

"Let's see what happens when Mr. Finkelman hears about your behavior. Let's see what he does when you explain why you walked off this picture."

A chill sensation crawled over Dominic from the back of his neck to the base of his spine. He thought about his vindictive agent and the grisly tales concerning some of Bernie's former clients. The man was implicated in at least three deaths, wasn't he? There were probably more, and God knows what else. He was a man with blood on his hands.

What would that nasty bastard do if Dominic quit the picture and arrived at Bernie's office asking for further work? The image of the old man's grotesque Windsor cane popped into his head, making him shudder. Bernie always seemed to be looking for an excuse to put his crude weapon to use, and if Dominic's exploits cost him money, he would surely corner his client, wielding that wooden baton like a master Jedi.

"That's right," leered Ignacio, detecting anxiety in the young actor. "Now, back into position."

Despite fierce reluctance, remarkably, there wasn't a soul on the set willing to defy the director. In fact, the cameraman was incredibly obedient, and even Sebastián, who was a bag of jitters barely able to stand still, was unexpectedly meek and dutiful.

Dominic lumbered back to his mark, resigned to repeating the scene, come what may. Though safety was not a priority for Ignacio, Dominic could scarcely look at the pistol, let alone touch it. Thoughts of firing another bullet by accident made him nervous and distracted, with his physical performance more wooden than usual.

"Action," yelled Ignacio for the umpteenth time.

This time, Luis grabbed Dominic firmly by the collar,

elbowing him out of the way when he went for his gun. They tussled for a long time, with Dominic visibly unable, albeit secretly disinclined, to get near the man's firearm. Ignacio let the action run and run, watching them with exhilaration. Luis' hands were like giant slabs of meat, and when he fastened one around Dominic's mouth and pushed the actor's head back, Ignacio could see the pain welling in Dominic's eyes. He knew that shot would look terrific on the big screen and was elated that they were capturing this real-life battle on film.

Dominic wrestled an arm free and repeatedly pounded Luis on the head until Luis finally let go of him and put up an arm to protect himself. Immediately, Dominic grabbed the man's gun, snatching it from the holster. Luis instinctively batted the revolver out of Dominic's hand before he could clasp it properly. It leaped out of his grip, landing on the ground a few feet away.

Dominic threw himself at Luis, getting his hands around the man's neck. A split second later, a rock-hard fist caught him under the ribs, and as he lurched away, a second punch clipped him on the jaw. The landscape began to spin as he staggered backward, trying to keep his balance, and when a third blow connected with his chest, his legs buckled, and he found himself sitting on the ground, staring at the fuzzy outline of his fellow actor.

Luis approached him quickly and pulled him to his feet by his collar. He drew back his fist, poised to slam his knuckles into Dominic's face.

At that moment, Dominic thrust his head forward with force. It was malicious, heat-of-the-moment stuff provoked by Luis' unrepressed brutality. His forehead thumped Luis in the mouth, causing the bulky man to bellow and topple backward. His legs and arms flailed wildly as he fell, and he landed heavily on his back on the ground. Dirt kicked up as he struggled to get back on his feet.

Slightly dazed, Dominic staggered to the prostrate figure thrashing about in the dirt, sank down on one knee, and grabbed

Luis by the neck. He was so angry he wanted to crush the man's larynx.

As he went to deliver his line, he hesitated. Immobile, his mouth agape and his eyes straying toward the director in search of assistance, he desperately wondered: *What the hell is my line?*

Aware that the inconsiderate brute, Luis, had practically pounded all lucid sense out of him, his parched lips moved wordlessly as he fought to accurately articulate the scripted words. Then he gave a quick shake of the head to clear thoughts of pain from his mind. Recollections from his last rehearsal finally began to filter into his head.

He cleared his throat and said hoarsely, "You made a deal with Marcos and Fábio, didn't you?" He shook the man forcefully by the neck. "Who else is in on it? Who are the other crooked cops?"

"Go to hell!" croaked Luis.

Dominic pretended to give him a heavy crack on the head with his fist. It required all his resolve not to hit him for real. "What did you do with María, you scumbag?"

Luis spat at him. "*Vete a la mierda, hijo de puta.*"

Dominic pushed Luis' head away and got to his feet. He walked over to where the gun lay and picked it up. "You'll answer every one of my questions," he demanded, pointing the gun at Luis, "or you'll die slowly, painfully, wishing you had not been so stubborn."

"Cut," yelled Ignacio after a lengthy silence. "Print it."

Dominic lowered the gun, feeling totally exhausted. His finger strayed so far from the trigger that it made his hand hurt.

"Magnificent!" said Ignacio delightedly. "Dominic, Luis, you have excelled yourselves. That was the best take yet. Dominic, those long pauses were wonderful, just wonderful. You see how good we can be when we go off script."

Off-script might not be so bad, as some of the dialogue stank worse than month-old garbage. No wonder he was having a hard time remembering his lines. He feared that his ghastly efforts in the last scene might help secure the film a Golden Raspberry Award for Worst Picture.

A girl came forward carrying a makeup bag. Dominic was so tired he wanted to fall into her arms. She brushed him down and started to apply his makeup.

Ignacio gestured to the cameraman. "Okay, we will do the close-up shots now. Come on. Let's get things moving faster."

The girl dabbed hastily at Dominic's lip. The way Dominic's face throbbed, he was sure it wouldn't be long before his cheek and lip started to swell up.

Maybe I'm not cut out for action pictures, he thought miserably. *Perhaps radio ads aren't so bad after all.*

He gazed at Ignacio despairingly, deliberating how to vacate the picture. He wondered if the only way off this set was if something happened to the director. Something tragic.

As he contemplated the various ways to get back to Hollywood and the small-time acting life he once sought to advance, his gaze slowly drifted to the handgun and the chamber containing live rounds.

Eleven

THAT gorgeous, whopping four-poster bed seemed to sing him a lullaby when he stepped into his hotel room late that evening. The fresh, crisp sheets looked welcoming, and a piece of rich chocolate in shiny foil sat on one of the plump pillows. The only thing missing was a buxom maid in her negligee inviting him beneath the covers.

He slept long and deeply, dreaming he was back in his apartment in LA. His muscles were so tired his body barely stirred during the night. He didn't want to budge from his position in the bed, not even when his alarm clock went off. In fact, he slept through the alarm, the noisy chime not registering in his mind. It was the hotel telephone on the bedside table that jerked him awake. The sound of Maria Romero's surly voice reminding him to get out of bed undermined his blissful demeanor. He lied that he had been awake for hours and was about to head to the lobby. Politely bidding her goodbye, through gritted teeth, he returned the receiver to its cradle with savage force.

"This movie is killing me," he muttered.

His mind was on the director's dodgy methods rather than the early starts. *Real stunts, real bullets.* He shuddered at the notion. The movie's title felt like an indication of what was to come, and he wished to God that Jules Fern at Griffin Pictures had never uttered his name to Ignacio's assistant. *A Bullet for Silver Face.* "Christ, what a title!" he said, now believing that the said bullet was headed for his shiny face.

He grabbed his copy of the shooting script and flipped through the pages for twenty minutes. His upcoming scenes were a nerve-jangling series of set pieces, and the thought of them made him want to get under the covers. *Real stunts, real bullets.* It was enough to bring Dominic to his knees in prayer. He wasn't the religious type and chose not to contemplate the existence of a higher power, and yet, in times of great stress, he became a true believer. The heavy book in the top drawer of his dresser, which he had hoped was the Kama Sutra but which turned out to be a bible, compelled him to repent for an almost exhaustive catalog of sins. Casting aside his shooting script, he cowed at the foot of his bed, murmuring hysterically about the value of his life and his longing to do more good deeds. Panic and fear of his impending death had reduced him to a sniveling wreck.

A sincere promise to do God's work backed up his tearful plea for more time on earth, and by the time he was finished, his eyes smarted, and his voice was hoarse. A cramp in his calf meant it took him some time to get to his feet, and then he promptly sat down on his bed, needing time to recuperate. He was jittery and experiencing twinges of pain throughout his body. Unaccustomed to the rigors of an Ignacio Martinez picture, his muscles screamed for a reprieve; as he meditated on the inevitable horrors in store for him that day, he clutched the corner of the comforter, twisting the material tightly in his fist. Though he had been awake for twenty minutes, he longed for the day to be over.

Ignacio gave Dominic a dirty look when the actor arrived on the set that morning. "What's the matter?"

The dark circles under Dominic's eyes were more prominent than before. The twitch in his eye was barely perceptible, but it was there, nonetheless.

"You look like you haven't slept for a week. Are we not providing you with sufficient accommodation?"

Dominic put his hands up in surrender. "I've no complaints.

The accommodation is excellent."

Ignacio harrumphed. "Sofía tells me you have a luxury suite."

"For now."

"I didn't know the production company had booked you a suite."

"They didn't. The hotel gave me a complimentary upgrade."

"Sofía has complained to everyone on the crew about your room," said Ignacio, scowling. "She's insisting on a luxury suite of her own."

"Tell her she can have mine. My upgrade was temporary, and it's due to expire after tonight."

Ignacio's mood immediately improved. "Better go see Eliana. I want to start shooting in an hour."

"With a camera, I hope. I've dodged enough bullets this week."

"Is that so?" responded Ignacio without the slightest trace of humor.

"If we're going to use real bullets again, perhaps we should get outfitted with bulletproof vests."

"That's not a bad idea," said Ignacio, visibly peeved by the sarcastic remark. "A better idea is not to aim the gun at the assistant director's head next time you intend to pull the trigger."

Dominic retorted with embarrassment, "It was an accident."

"I should hope it was. All the same, exercise caution when you have a gun in your hand."

It was Dominic's turn to harrumph. He acknowledged the comment with a terse nod and headed off to find Eliana. Judging by the director's tetchy mood, he had a feeling he was about to experience another unpleasant day of work. His body was full of aches and pains caused by the excessive fight scenes and unwarranted stunt work. One more solid punch to his abdomen, and he might not have the strength or the will to get back up.

In the salon, he picked up the latest copy of *USA Today*, which had been procured specially for him, and settled into a chair. He shuddered as he skimmed through some of the stories.

Commuter plane returning from Cincinnati crashes into a snowy field and explodes on its approach to Detroit's Metropolitan Airport, killing the 29 aboard. Frank Sinatra hospitalized after suffering heart attack two days after being discharged from the hospital for an unspecified ailment.

Death and destruction and disease were the bywords for the day, with an intriguing case of industrial espionage offering respite from the doom and gloom: *Volkswagen agrees to pay General Motors $100 Million and buy $1 billion in GM parts to settle lawsuit alleging theft of trade secrets.*

There was one inspirational story among the headlines: *English yachtsman Tony Bullimore found alive after 5 days entombed in his upturned yacht in the arctic Southern Ocean.* Kept alive by a small amount of water and chocolate, he had somehow avoided a tragic end until his miraculous rescue. It was the sort of cheerful ending that Hollywood lapped up, and Dominic idly speculated which actor would land the role of the sailor.

Eliana stopped by with her makeup bag while he worked through the entertainment pages. Her close scrutiny of his face alarmed him.

"Are you ill?" she asked. "You look terrible."

"No, but thank you for that," he responded with mild displeasure.

"These heavy black circles around your eyes worry me."

He shrugged. "No need to worry. I'm just having trouble getting sleep, that's all."

"Stress?"

"Hell, yes. And I'm not getting enough sleep."

She wore a scornful expression. "I suggest you lay off the booze and the drugs. You will sleep better that way."

He turned a blind eye to the sarcasm. "Any gossip for me?"

She glanced over her shoulder to make sure they were not

being overheard. "Early this morning, Mister Óscar Chiosso came to the campus."

"Who?"

"The executive producer."

"Come to see the rushes, I imagine. Not exactly the gossip I meant. Anything juicier?"

"He was very angry. I heard him arguing with Ignacio."

"Do you know what about?"

"He had watched the first dailies and wasn't pleased with how the film was going."

"He's not griping about my performance, is he?"

"Who can say," she shrugged, not easing his mind. "All I know is that he threatened Ignacio. Said that he would have him replaced unless he made changes."

"What sort of changes?"

"I heard Mister Chiosso tell him that he didn't like the movie. Hated it, actually. He told Ignacio that this was not the movie that they commissioned. He complained that the movie's tone was too dark and the scenes too long. He had a script open in his hand while he picked apart the film. I saw him tear out several pages and throw them at Ignacio. 'This is too violent,' he said, and 'this will take too long to film.' Ignacio swore at him and tried to defend the scenes, but Mister Chiosso didn't seem satisfied by Ignacio's responses. They finally called a truce."

Dominic listened quietly, wondering how Óscar Chiosso's appearance would affect the picture.

"I'm sure we will hear more arguments between the two men," continued Eliana. "I sense an ugly situation is developing. Either Ignacio will back down and make changes, or he will soon leave the movie."

"Ignacio doesn't seem like the sort to back down," Dominic remarked gravely.

"Then we will be getting a new director."

———— ✦ ————

Exactly two hours later, he sat rigidly in the driver's seat of a red Renault 19, waiting for his cue, wondering when they would break for lunch. His shoulders felt tight, and his facial muscles throbbed. He wasn't conscious of his fingers tapping against the steering wheel.

If only the stunt car driver would take over, he thought, sick to death of being in the vehicle. He tried not to let his frustration show. Deep down, he was annoyed with Ignacio and angry with himself. They were up to take number twelve of what was, on paper, a straightforward action sequence. In actuality, it was a surprisingly tricky series of physically demanding feats that he wasn't sure he would ever get right. Ignacio could have saved himself a great deal of time if he had brought in a professional driver for the scene, but he was extremely keen for the audience to *see* Dominic perform the stunts.

Unfortunately, although Dominic was a lousy driver—reliably unobservant and with poor spatial awareness—his foot kneaded the gas pedal like a feeble old woman. What Ignacio wanted from him was the sort of thing he was ill-equipped to do: drive like a maniac. He was sure this was something that came naturally to the average Uruguayan. Dominic, though, was a relatively safe driver. Even when he drove fast, he drove defensively.

There was, of course, that little incident with the road sign on the interstate last summer… Though that wasn't entirely his fault. That blasted truck driver with the annoying bumper sticker was partly responsible, and so too was his agent.

"Bloody Bernie Finkelman," he grumbled.

Realizing that the director was giving him the signal to start the car, he turned the key in the ignition, put the car in gear, and jammed his foot on the accelerator. The car roared and jumped forward, juddering along the rough terrain. A thick cloud of dust billowed from under the tires as the vehicle gathered speed.

Through the swirl of filth, he saw the dense line of trees ahead and steered the car toward them until the last moment. Then he hit the brake and cranked the wheel, swerving out of the way of a thick tree trunk.

The wheels locked, and the car twirled harshly.

For a moment, he didn't know if he had hit the brake too hard or too late, and he clung to the steering wheel and gritted his teeth while the vehicle twirled one hundred and eighty degrees. His eyes watched the landscape rotate and puffs of soil gathered on the windows. He was braced for impact, almost expecting to hear the metal grate against a tree.

Eventually, the car skidded to a halt, and he was slammed into the door panel. His head banged against the window, though thankfully, it didn't cause him much pain. He recovered quickly and cut the engine. The only noise he heard was the sound of fragments of earth raining down on the chassis. He breathed unsteadily, feeling the muscles in his shoulders slacken slightly.

Then, a bullet pinged off the hood.

The technicians had pre-made holes, placed squibs in them, then filled them back over and re-painted them. Small explosive charges, placed inside little holders to help focus the blast outward, were set off electronically. Decals from the special effects team would then be added later.

Dominic hunkered down in his seat as two more firecracker explosives burst in quick succession.

Hurriedly, he tugged on the door handle and threw his shoulder against the door. He felt a sudden throb of pain and instantly regretted having done it, knowing he would have a mean-looking bruise in the morning to add to his other collection of injuries.

The door swung open, and he spilled out of the car, falling headfirst onto the ground. As he scrambled away from the vehicle, keeping low, two more gunshots rang out. One slug smacked against the passenger side door, and the other whistled over his head.

He staggered and slumped face down in the grass. Scurrying along on all fours, he tucked himself into a tight ball behind the front wheel. His heart was pounding, and he could scarcely breathe. He wasn't sure what was real and what was a special effect. Knowing the effort required to set up the effects, he knew the director would be furious if multiple takes were needed. He also knew that although the effects looked awesome, they came with associated safety issues should anyone be standing too close to them.

Dominic hoped to God the director wasn't fool enough to use real bullets. He didn't trust Luis' aim.

His costar hollered his dialogue with manic zeal. "Come out from behind the car, Pucker."

Though out of breath, Dominic managed to find his voice. In a hoarse cry, he delivered his godawful line as clearly as he could. "Go to hell!"

"After you, Pucker. I can shoot at you all day."

"Yeah? Well, you're a lousy shot," bawled Dominic in an unsteady voice.

He felt sure there was some truth in the words.

"Maybe so, but all the same, I have plenty of time and plenty of bullets."

His gun fired again, the bullet intended to go harmlessly wide, and Dominic automatically tucked his head between his legs, shielding his head with his arms.

Cowering by the side of the car, praying metal or painted plastic wouldn't hit him, Dominic had difficulty focusing on the scene. He was thankful he had delivered his two lines of dialogue. He wasn't sure his nerves would hold for another take.

"Hold tight. I'm coming for you, Pucker."

Dominic heard Luis reloading his pistol, and it terrified him. That was his cue to get the hell away from the car.

He got to his feet and started to run. The scene had been set up to allow him plenty of time to get far away from the car before the technicians blew it to smithereens. Unfortunately, his tired legs stopped him from making it to the shelter of the trees. Barely twenty feet from the vehicle, his foot landed in a sizeable divot, and as he stumbled, the right toe of his boot clipped his left heel, causing the left shoe to come off. He was instantly thrown off balance and pitched face-first into the grass. His forehead took the brunt of the impact, thudding into the earth and leaving an impression.

It took a moment before the pain registered in his brain, and when he lifted his head, he felt the ground begin to whirl. He used his sleeve to wipe dirt from his face, but his vision remained fuzzy. Realizing the danger, he pulled himself upright. All he could see was a green haze.

He lumbered on, worried about ruining the take if he lingered, hoping he was moving in the right direction. He only managed a few awkward strides, and then the ground beneath him trembled, and there was a thunderous explosion behind him.

Twelve

HE saw the ball of flame rise into the air. Black smoke billowed from what was left of the wrecked automobile.

Ignacio's voice came in loud and clear over the megaphone. "Cut! Print it. Thank you, everybody. I appreciate the hard work. That's going to be a great scene."

Dominic heard cheers go up, and the crew members began to applaud. He couldn't believe his luck; he couldn't believe he was still in one piece.

Sometimes, the best moments were the impromptu ones. Dominic was aware that his mistakes in the last take had led things to veer off-script, but the fact that he had bungled his way through it without displeasing the director encouraged him tremendously. There was hope yet that he might not live to regret making the picture.

He walked toward the small ensemble of people who made up the film crew. His stride was sluggish, and his legs and arms ached. Bullets, explosions and bare-knuckle fistfights were continual, disconcerting distractions, and trying to remember lines while worried about being blown to smithereens was an eternal challenge. This newest situation threatened to undermine his competency as an actor.

He approached the director, eager to voice his concerns about safety but strategizing the most tactful way to do it. That last scene had taxed him greatly, exhausting him emotionally and physically. In fact, he felt like he had aged a couple of years in one day. For all his running, fighting, shooting, and driving, these three scenes only accounted for a few minutes of screen time.

He opened his mouth to speak, but the director got the first word. "Every time the camera rolls, you get better and better, Dominic." He clamped a hand on the actor's shoulder. "You were born to be an action star. It was a great idea to use live ammunition, don't you think?"

"Christ, no! I've been scared out of my wits all morning," admitted Dominic, looking agitated.

"Exactly! You might be a good actor, but I don't think I could get that authentically scared reaction out of you if we used blanks."

"What about safety, dammit? One of us might be killed or injured?"

There was a mischievous twinkle in Ignacio's eyes. "Ah, yes. Wouldn't that be something? Think how it would look on film. Ha! There would be no need for special effects and gory makeup, yes? And what about all the publicity that catastrophes generate? Think of those average pictures that became cult classics. *The Crow*, for instance. Death on a film set often turns a decent performance into a legendary one."

There were goosebumps on Dominic's arms. A lead actor in his prime had tragically lost his life because of an improperly prepared prop gun. Disconcertingly, Ignacio seemed to have misinterpreted the message regarding safety.

"I'm not sure I want to become legendary. Not if it means I have to die to obtain that distinction."

"Yes. What good is fame when you are dead? You cannot profit from all those good newspaper headlines, can you? Dying famously results in you getting laid in style—laid to rest."

While Ignacio laughed heartily at his own joke, Dominic managed not to roll his eyes.

"Seriously, Dominic, don't fret so much. The worst is over.

We have put away the guns for today. And let me tell you, what we have done so far looks wonderful."

"That's a blessing."

"We'll break for lunch now. This afternoon, we shoot some scenes between you and Sofía."

With no explosions or gunplay planned, Dominic felt better about how the afternoon would play out. It wasn't until the fourth take of his first scene with Sofía that he realized the afternoon might be no less perilous than the morning.

"Cut! Cut! Cut!" Ignacio angrily yelled. "The scene is supposed to have romance in it. Is there no romance in you, Dominic? Is a woman purely a means of sexual gratification? You're supposed to listen to what Sofía tells you—listen with interest, not wait for her lips to stop moving. And when you kiss her, do it tenderly, not passionately."

Dominic let out a heavy groan and put a hand through his hair. The makeup artist immediately came jogging up to him and started adjusting his hair to get it back to its original state. Ignacio continued his lecture while she squirted hairspray and moved the hair about with a comb.

"Perhaps we can concentrate less on the kiss and more on the interaction between you two. Look her in the eye and listen to her voice. Think about the words pouring sweetly from her mouth. Right now, your thoughts are elsewhere—as are your eyes." The blank look on Dominic's face made him twist his lips in annoyance. "For God's sake, man. Keep your hands off her ass and your eyes off her breasts."

By the end of the next take, Ignacio had lost all patience with the actor. He walked over to Dominic, a stern expression on his face and his hands clenched into fists. "I think you connect closely with your character, but I'm not sure you understand Bruce's relationship with María."

He then launched into a ten-minute discourse on the role of María and the importance of Dominic breathing life into their interactions. Dominic listened without saying a word. He hadn't been able to instill much passion into his performance, partly because a slight awkwardness existed between the two actors. Partly, he was just plain tired.

When Ignacio returned to his position behind the camera, Dominic shook off his lethargy and discovered the allusion of passion the part demanded. The rapid transformation was impressive, and during the ensuing take, Sofía found herself hypnotized by his handsome, smoldering eyes, which seemed to gleam with ardor for her, and confident from the kiss that ended the scene that his craving for her was earnest and the tenderness in his voice devoid of pretense. She knew he wasn't *that* good an actor.

As for Dominic, the moment their lips touched, it felt like time had stopped. The feel of her lustful hands exploring his back and the sensation of her affectionate body pressed against his provoked a stirring in his loins. He relished her succulent lower lip and the faint, sweet scent of her breath. Once more, she had become the hungry, licentious creature of sensual pleasure he had blissfully explored during the night they met. Again, she filled him with overwhelming desire, and he yearned for another undisturbed nighttime encounter.

He forgot all about the camera, the director, and the various members of the film crew standing close by like voyeurs, silently beholding an unseemly moment of private passion between two lovers.

Eventually, Sofía released her grip on Dominic and inched her body away from his, instantly leaving him with a sense of profound sadness. When she delivered her lines, bringing the scene to a close, he felt as if he had been wrenched too soon from a happy dream. He watched her intently, trying to discern if she bore strong feelings for him or not. Her potent yearning for him had dissipated all too rapidly, and no telltale signs of affection lingered in her eyes. The unexpected coolness in her manner undermined his seesawing confidence, provoking unwarranted negativity and a desperate wish to feel wanted.

While Dominic stared at her despairingly, keen for a further take, the director rose hurriedly from his seat. "Cut!" he roared.

Both actors turned toward him, startled by the harshness in his tone. The fierce lines on Ignacio's reddened face made it clear to everyone that he was brimming with fury.

"Print it!" he snarled.

And without another word, he stormed off the set.

———— ✦ ————

"If you're free later, perhaps we could go for a drink?" Sofía boldly proposed later that day.

Dominic was taken aback. Earlier, he sensed antipathy, but he determined a softening toward him as she looked at him now. Though he couldn't quite fathom the warmth in her, he nevertheless appreciated it. "That sounds nice."

"Not your place again, though," she clarified. "I know a better place nearby that serves great wine."

"Sure. But I'm not really a wine drinker. I wouldn't know the difference between a good wine and a glass of prune juice."

She shrugged. "*I'll* pick out some good wines for you. You can just sample the many wines and offer an opinion."

"I'll take you up on the invitation. But I wonder if it's a good idea. People say I'm too fond of both those things."

She gave him a toothy smile. "I hardly think it would be a problem. A man who likes to drink and has something interesting to say usually works out fine."

"Even if you don't like what he has to say?"

She smirked. "A few more drinks will usually fix that problem."

He laughed. It was his first moment of gaiety in days.

She said the bar's name and told him she would be there from eight o'clock onwards.

Later, he stopped briefly at the reception desk and asked the elderly man behind the desk for directions to the bar. "Is it far?" he asked.

The old man adjusted his thick glasses and peered closely at the piece of paper as though the writing were microscopic. He vigorously shook his head, and his glasses almost slid off his face, and then he pulled out a street map and explained the route in great detail. With extensive use of his hands, he signaled which roads went where and what was sold in the various buildings along the street. Dominic felt he could have done without the geographical lesson but thanked him, all the same, and headed out of the hotel, quickly finding the street he was looking for, wishing he hadn't wasted time asking for directions. Hurriedly, he made his way down a street named Costa Rica. The bar Sofía had recommended was a few hundred meters away, and he was there within minutes.

He pushed open the heavy door and found himself in a stylish tavern with decorative soft white lights set into the walls and candelabras on the tables. Plenty of trendy young people were at the tables and booths, and loud chatter drowned out the instrumental music playing in the background. He headed toward the bar, licking his parched lips, more eager to taste alcohol than to see Sofía again. As he glanced about, unable to spot her, he wondered if she had come and gone already, figuring she'd been stood up.

As he beckoned the barman over, the woman perched on a stool to his left caught his eye. She had her back to him but turned her head when she heard his voice.

"Dominic, finally, you're here."

"Forgive me. I'm rather late."

He walked over to her at once. She stood up and surprised him by uninhibitedly wrapping her arms around him.

"I thought you might have forgotten our date," she said, kissing him lightly.

As he bent forward to give her a dry peck on the cheek, she moved her head at the exact moment, and they clonked heads.

"I'm so sorry," he said, feeling like a clumsy oaf.

They sat at the bar, and he looked at the wine glass on the counter in front of her. Her fingers were resting on the stem of the glass. "What are you drinking?"

"Preludio."

He observed the small splash of bright purple liquid in her glass. "You recommend it?" he asked, wondering if she was drinking it because it was fashionable or because she genuinely liked it.

"Yes. It's a premium wine under the Familia Deicas name. It's the best Uruguayan red you can drink."

"I'll have the same," he told the barman, pointing to her glass. "And another for the lady."

"Thank you," she said, patting his arm. "I think you'll enjoy it. It has hints of ripe forest fruits and a touch of ink."

He laughed. "I had a fountain pen as a boy, and ink squirted in my face once when I refilled it. I can't say I really liked the inky taste."

The barman set two clean glasses in front of them and delicately poured the wine, which had a slight violet tone.

Dominic brought the wine glass to his nose and breathed in the aroma. "Dried figs, red ripe fruits, and…what is that? Hm. Vanilla, I'd say. A fascinating blend of fragrances. Well, bottoms up, as they say."

Their glasses clinked together, and he took a big mouthful rather than sip it.

"You like it?" she asked him, smiling with satisfaction.

"God, yes. I can't detect any hint of ink, though."

"I can't, either. I went on a wine-tasting tour last year. The guide talked about the allusion of forest fruits and the faint taste of ink," she confessed. "When I tried the wine, I wasn't aware of anything like that. It must be that my taste buds are not sensitive enough to detect such things."

"I know the feeling. My taste buds are shot to hell. However, my sense of smell is still highly tuned. By the way, what is that gorgeous perfume you're wearing? Vol de Nuit?"

She rolled her eyes. "It's Champs Elysees, also by Guerlain."

"I was close, then."

Her expression suggested she thought the two fragrances were nothing alike. "This line of perfume was launched quite recently."

"Suits you."

He guzzled the rest of his drink and beckoned to the barman once he had set his glass on the counter.

"I'll have more wine, too," she told him, quaffing the rest of her drink.

He indicated two to the barman.

"Tell me more about yourself, Dominic. It's not every day I sit with the next big movie star."

"I'm hardly that," he snorted.

"You're the lead in Ignacio's movie. By all accounts, it will generate much buzz out here."

He silently watched the barman set clean wine glasses before them and pour their drinks. Though he was the principal actor in *A Bullet for Silver Face*, he felt like a charlatan. This was far from the gentility of Hollywood. It was grainy, vulgar, and daunting, and he hated it.

"I'm just a small-time actor," he confessed. "An unknown all-American face in a small foreign picture."

She puckered her lips and tilted her head to one side. "For now, perhaps, but that will change one day. Besides, your face will be well-known in Uruguay when the movie opens."

He shrugged as if to say big deal and reached for his drink.

"You think it's unimportant," she said, seeing his condescending look. "Many actors in the country would love to be in your shoes. They wouldn't think so lowly of the picture."

"Fair point," he said, realizing how conceited he must appear to her. He returned the glass to his lips and glugged the wine. He was too thirsty to savor it.

"What are your thoughts on that scene we did earlier today?" A frown appeared on his face, making her add, "We had chemistry, don't you think?"

It pleased him to hear her say it. The excitement she stirred in him during that scene was intense and startling, and her abrupt indifference afterward severely pinched his heartstrings. He no longer trusted his emotions.

"The kiss certainly went well, even if it upset Ignacio."

"It was more than that. I saw the look in your eyes, Dominic. That wasn't an act. Your emotions were genuine. I swear I could see love in your eyes."

He clicked his tongue. "Isn't that what the scene called for?"

"Admit it, Dominic," she said arrogantly. "You're in love with me."

He snickered. "Love is a strong word."

She nodded in agreement. There was wickedness in her eyes, though, and a look that warned him to be careful.

"Tell me something else about you," she begged. "I know so little except your appetite for action movies. What's the real Dominic Graves like?" She ran a finger playfully along his left cheek. "What kind of unpleasant creature lurks behind this sweet face?"

He chuckled softly. "It's not pretty. Deep down on the inside, there's a restless, self-centered rogue trying to escape—the vain, obnoxious, spiteful type who surfaces almost daily, for a few hours at a time."

She made a clicking sound with her tongue. "Sounds very much like every man. Doesn't really tell me much about Dominic Graves, does it?"

"It tells you quite a bit, actually." He put down his glass and leaned an elbow on the bar. "It tells you that I like to perform, that I like an audience. And look what it is I actually do for a living." He gave a derisive laugh and a little shake of the head. "I pull faces and commit to memory other people's philosophies and perspectives, try to pass them off as my own. When I'm not trying to convince people I'm somebody else, I'm trying to come to terms with who I really am. Sometimes, I feel like I've stripped away the very essence of my identity. I've become a blank canvas—a faceless, voiceless entity awaiting an owner. At the drop of a hat, I'll transform myself into whomever you want, and I'll stay that person for as long as you like. As long as the price is right."

"You can't be serious?" she said, slightly confused. "That's how you think of yourself?"

He took another pull on his drink. "It's difficult to put distance between the personal and the professional. They merge as one very quickly. Whether acting or auditioning, I'm forever incorporating someone else's viewpoint and mannerisms and striving to become a different Dominic for the day. Truth be told, there's not much substance to Dominic Graves. The role of an actor has practically consumed me."

"Garbage," she said sharply. "You're trying hard to convince me and yourself that you're an empty vessel, but I know better. You have many character traits, and you can't rid yourself of them."

He went to take another swig of wine, then realized his glass was empty. He signaled to the barman for another drink.

"Maybe I can help you strip away those negative thoughts you seem intent on carrying with you," she offered. "It's something I'm good at."

He eyed her lasciviously. "Is it now?"

"Among other things."

"In that case, I'm all yours."

A moment later, her hand was on the back of his neck, pushing his head down, making his lips meet hers. Her lips were warm and full and filled with desire. Eventually, her grip slackened, and he could come up for air.

"Why don't we go somewhere more discrete?" she advised.

He was in total agreement. "My canopy bed is to die for. Come on, let's go."

He swiftly paid for their drinks and led her out of the bar, eager to get her to his room before the alcohol wore off.

Thirteen

THE routine morning call from Maria Romero made sure he was up in time for work. His heavy-handedness with the telephone roused Sofía from sleep, and she pushed a small section of the bedsheet aside and swept tangles of hair from her face. "I feel exhausted," she rasped, struggling to push herself into a sitting position. "What time is it?"

As the sheet fell away, Dominic stared, entranced by her nakedness. Though petite, the bosoms were impeccably made. Before he could clasp them, she adjusted the sheet, covering herself up.

He was finally able to meet her gaze. "The time? Seven o'clock."

She tossed back the sheet and climbed out of bed, muttering, "I'm not getting enough sleep."

Her clothes were scattered across the floor. She gathered them up hurriedly. He watched her dress, unconcerned about his own tardiness.

"God knows how you're able to survive," she said, scowling at him while she fastened her bra strap. "You're practically on the set for the entire day."

Truth be told, he would have breathed a sigh of relief if they had fired him. He didn't have the courage to walk away from the project, and the thought of facing Bernie, should he break his contract, gave him the heebie-jeebies.

"I'm exhausted every day," he admitted. "Overworked and scared shitless."

She dressed hastily, indifferent to the fact he was watching her intently.

"It's early days. Expect it to get much tougher," she warned.

"Is that even possible?"

She stopped buttoning her skirt and staring at him coldly. "Ignacio isn't one to slow down or take a day off. You need to get used to the work schedule. There's still time for him to get a different lead actor. One that isn't afraid of hard work."

———◆———

On the set that afternoon, Ignacio approached Dominic while he was pacing outside the entrance to the college campus. "Here," he said, offering him a packet of cigarettes.

"No thanks," said Dominic, waving them away. "I don't smoke."

"Take it," Ignacio persisted, thrusting the carton into Dominic's hand. "Smoke a couple now before we rehearse the scene."

"I can't stand the taste or the smell," Dominic explained. "They make me gag."

"These are excellent cigarettes. They won't make you sick."

Dominic was eager to be rid of them, but as he tried to pass the packet back to Ignacio, the director casually evaded his outstretched hand, saying, "You'll need them for the scene. I want you to acquire a taste for this brand."

"That won't happen. Cigars are the worst, but pipes of all kinds make me nauseous, and cigarettes affect me just as much. Even the herbal kind."

"Bruce Pucker is a smoker. He drinks hard, works hard, and plays hard."

"Three out of four ain't bad," muttered Dominic.

The remark didn't mollify Ignacio. "Pucker would be a chain smoker if only he had the time. Think of him as a man walking a fine line between success and a nervous breakdown. He's a flourishing journalist for a big national newspaper who stays up late most nights frantically trying to hit his deadlines. He's bound up by stress, and he relieves his tension by drinking copious amounts of coffee and liquor and puffing away at a cigarette. One day, he will win the Pulitzer Prize. Though he might die from a heart attack first."

Dominic glanced down at the packet of Fortaleza in his hand. "I don't see why he has to smoke. My voice isn't gruff enough to make the audience believe I'm a heavy smoker."

"Never mind your voice," snapped Ignacio. "I want you to look comfortable with a cigarette between your fingers."

"That will take a lot of work."

Ignacio looked fit to explode. "You're an actor, for Christ's sake! Act like you know how to smoke."

Shaken by Ignacio's angry outburst, Dominic hurriedly tore the seal off the packet of cigarettes, took one out, and put it in his mouth. He stared at Ignacio expectantly, and the director promptly pulled a matchbook from his pocket. Dominic spotted the hotel's logo on the cover. Ignacio had picked it up in the restaurant bar when they dined together.

Ignacio tore a match from the book, slid the match head along the striker, and lit Dominic's cigarette. Dominic managed one long draw before he started to cough. His coughing fit lasted almost a full minute.

He had gotten the cough under control when they started filming, but on the third take, his face turned ashen, and he frenziedly pushed his way past the other actors. After staggering slightly, he dropped to the ground, crawling on all fours, gagged, then vomited.

Óscar Chiosso, who had been lurking unseen in the background, stepped forward. "What are you trying to do to this actor? Kill him? Clearly, he can't handle a cigarette. You're making him ill and wasting time."

"I don't want your advice. I'm trying to film here. We have a lot to get through, so let me get on with it," urged Ignacio, reigning in his temper. "Dominic, I have an idea."

Dominic wiped his mouth with his sleeve and struggled to his feet. He turned around and faced Ignacio, swaying a little.

"Instead of smoking the cigarette, perhaps you can simply hold it."

Dominic took a deep breath. The pungent smell of tobacco was still in the air, making him queasy. He tried not to think about it.

"Okay," he said, unsure if he could stomach the smell but willing to try it anyway. "Do you want it lit or unlit?"

"Lit," said Ignacio. He pretended not to notice the vomit on Dominic's shoes.

During the next take, Dominic cursed softly in the middle of his line and flapped his hand like he had been stung.

Ignacio's voice boomed out, "Cut! What's the matter now?"

Dominic looked embarrassed. "I burned my finger on the cigarette."

Óscar Chiosso groaned and kicked a clump of dirt in annoyance.

Ignacio chewed angrily on his bottom lip, trying to mask his frustration. "Okay, back into position. Let's try it again."

Dominic took the packet of cigarettes from his pocket and fumbled a cigarette into his mouth. When he attempted to light it, Óscar Chiosso hollered, "You have the wrong cigarette end in your mouth!"

It took until take the twenty-eighth take before Ignacio was satisfied with the scene. When Dominic walked off the set, he heard Chiosso and Ignacio at it again, bickering with one another over the merits of the scene.

They looked like they were squaring off for a fight, and the aggression in their faces intimated it would be an incredibly bloody punch-up.

Fourteen

THE tranquility of the college campus ended days later as filming shifted gear, focusing on busy street scenes and city landscapes. Dominic perked up when he examined his call sheet and saw they would be filming in more lively locations throughout the city. He craved a change of scene.

He woke before his alarm call, showered, dressed, and breakfasted before six o'clock. Then, sick of sitting on his bed, twiddling his thumbs, he went to the lobby to wait for his taxi.

A short man with wiry black hair, casually dressed in faded jeans and a stained t-shirt, stepped into the lobby. He loudly announced the name written on the slip of paper in his hand: "Dommy Gave."

Dominic chuckled, quite liking the novel variation on his name.

"Yes, that's me," he responded, getting to his feet.

"Good morning, sir. I am Eduardo. I come to pick you up."

He signaled with his thumb for Dominic to follow him and then exited the hotel briskly, never once looking back, making his way to his car with steely determination.

Dominic hurried after him, stepping outside in time to see Eduardo climb into the driver's seat of a black and yellow car with a light sign and the word *taxi* on top. He jogged to the car, pulled open the back door, and got in speedily. Had he moved any faster, people might have presumed they were watching two crooks absconding in a getaway car.

He reached over to shut the door and was surprised to see Sofía standing by the curb.

"Hold on! Wait for me," she said breathlessly.

He moved over to let her in, wondering if she had been in the lobby the whole time and why he hadn't noticed her.

"You weren't going to wait for me," she grumbled, highly annoyed at him.

He gave a contrite shrug. "I didn't know you were coming."

She harrumphed. "More like you didn't want me to ride with you."

"Not at all. Why should I care?"

"You're hurt I didn't come to your room last night."

He made a derisive sound with his lips. If anything, he was pleased about the extra sleep he had been able to grab. "You shouldn't feel like you have to warm my bed every night."

She didn't take kindly to the remark. "I *don't* feel like I have to. Thought I was doing you a favor, actually."

"A favor, huh."

"Don't feign indifference. Your feelings for me are unmistakable. And now you're hurt. Hurt because I didn't pay you some attention yesterday."

He gazed out of the window, trying to hide his irritation.

"Ha. Now you're pouting," she observed gleefully. "I see I've bruised your delicate sense of pride."

"You haven't bruised anything."

Not this time, he thought, recalling her brutal whack to his head. He stared at the picturesque landscape with slitted eyes, singed by her roasting comments. *Pouting, indeed! What a high opinion she had of herself. And what a low opinion she had of him!*

He heard her sigh and imagined her rolling her eyes and shaking her head. Quite frankly, he couldn't bring himself to look at her. Evidently, he had allowed her to claim proprietorship of him at some point. He was now Sofía's paramour, beholden to her for the duration of his stay in Uruguay and expected to play the doting lover, chasing after her affections. Only, Dominic wasn't the chasing kind, and his costars were not love interests outside of the cinema screen. He didn't pout unless it was stated in the film script. Her belief that he pined for her at night was pure fantasy. She was merely a pleasant distraction, nothing more. And the more he thought on that, the more he questioned the wisdom of encouraging anything beyond civility. Another night of passion, though an otherwise bearable proposition, was fraught with peril. A tender kiss, though harmless on the film set during a take, might prove a grave mistake if it happened more than once and if Ignacio got wind of it. Was it prudent to covet the beautiful partner of a protective, gun-toting director who was titillated by the thought of one of his actors dying, for real, on celluloid?

Dominic rode the taxi in silence, deliberating how to quietly extinguish Sofía's affection for him but preserve their smoldering on-screen chemistry. For one of the few times in his life, he cursed his acting abilities, regretting his tremendous portrayal of a man in love. But he was confident he could soon remedy the situation. If his considerable acting prowess was such that he could make an actress who disliked him fall wholly in love with him during a take, then it was feasible that he could achieve the reverse. Sweet and charming and adorable though he was, it was his duty to make Sofía realize her obligations to Ignacio and bury her private desires for the sake of their careers.

When the taxi dropped them downtown, Dominic and Sofía made their way a few hundred feet to where Ignacio and the crew gathered. As they approached, Dominic observed a dozen or so people scurrying about, setting up equipment. Ignacio scooted around them, looking through the square shape he had formed with his hands as if framing a shot. Sofía approached the assistant director and lightly tapped him on the shoulder. Sebastián was typically a crabby man whom Dominic tended to avoid, but when he turned around and saw Sofía, he welcomed her with a smile.

Dominic moved away from them, turning his attention to the street, which was full of noise and activity, with bystanders already gathering on the sidewalks. The morning shoot would be a succession of short scenes, with Dominic featuring in practically all of them. Setting up each shot would be the most time-consuming aspect.

He traipsed up and down the sidewalk for several minutes, casually observing the hard-working film crew, savoring the fleeting moment of harmony. Typically, there would be a knot of nervous excitement in the pit of his stomach when he arrived on a movie set. He would hear anxious, garbled exchanges, and while people scuttled past him with equipment, there would be a hoarse voice in the background barking orders and redirecting foot traffic. The general hustle and bustle around him would inevitably add to his nervousness. Oddly, he felt cheerful, composed, and utterly unaffected by the commotion around him this time.

When Sofía stopped chit-chatting with Sebastián and returned to Dominic's side, he jumped when her cold fingers touched his wrist. He was absorbed in a copy of the shooting script, mastering his lines.

"Sebastián says Ignacio and Óscar had a giant argument this morning," she said apprehensively.

"Over what exactly?"

"I'll show you," she said, commandeering his script.

She flipped through the pages, pointing to the scene.

"How ridiculous," he scoffed, thinking it an innocuous passage. "What on earth is there to quarrel about?"

"Óscar doesn't like the humor."

"What's his complaint?"

"I'm supposed to yell at you in a shrill voice and stamp my foot in a sulky way, but Óscar thinks the way I scream at you is cartoonish. He told Ignacio that if my yell was over-the-top, it would mar the rest of my performance."

Dominic shrugged dismissively. He felt confident she would pull off the scene without a hitch. Though not a great actress, she had a terrific shriek, and it seemed far from cartoonish. Nevertheless, he candidly remarked, "How loud are you going to shout?"

"Loud, but not so loud that it hurts your ears."

"I like the idea of that. However, the script says shrill."

"I know what it says in the script."

"You're going to do it high-pitched?"

"Yes. I want to squawk the line."

"Show me."

She balked at the idea, and with an offhand shrug, he muttered, "As long as you know how you want to do it."

"I know how I want to do it. I'm just worried that acting out the scene the way it's written might not be good for me. I don't want my character to come across as deranged."

"I'm sure the scene will be fine."

"Maybe the script needs to be changed."

Dominic's face twitched with anxiety. "Let Ignacio shoot it the way the scriptwriter intended," he urged, concerned about script changes.

"But what if Óscar is right? What if I sound ridiculous?"

"He can edit it out if it doesn't seem in context with the rest of the movie."

"And if Ignacio doesn't edit out the scene?" she persisted. "I don't want people to mock my performance."

"Ignacio knows what he's doing," Dominic insisted, though he didn't know if he believed it.

"Yes, yes, of course," she agreed vociferously but visibly skeptical.

"Was that all they discussed?" he asked, wanting to steer the conversation away from script rewrites. "You said they had a giant argument."

Learning new lines never bothered him. However, he feared that Sofía's complaints about the scene would have an adverse effect, particularly on his screen time.

"Sebastián said that the dispute turned physical. And he's not prone to exaggeration."

"All that huffing and puffing over a trivial scene like that," snorted Dominic. "How did the argument end?"

"Óscar wouldn't back down. He was insistent that Ignacio shoot the scene differently. That's when Ignacio got rough with him."

"Rough?" said Dominic, full of concern.

"Grabbed him by the throat."

"Christ!"

"I don't think Óscar said a word. He turned red in the face and looked petrified."

"Incapacitated, I imagine," muttered Dominic, aghast. "What happened then?"

"Ignacio threatened to kill him if he undermined him again."

"Holy crap!" murmured Dominic, wishing he had been there to witness it.

"Then he threw Óscar aside and stormed off."

Dominic gazed past Sofía, his eyes fixedly assessing Ignacio, who seemed perfectly calm now. He knew Ignacio could be a bit irrational sometimes, but he had yet to see the man thoroughly lose his temper. He hoped he never would, either.

"Did he apologize to Óscar later?"

"No."

Dominic wondered how much more insolence Óscar Chiosso would absorb before he took measures to see that Ignacio was fired. It seemed like it would be only a matter of time before the hot-tempered director got his marching orders.

Fifteen

FOR days, the mood on the set was incredibly unpleasant, with the director and producer continually squabbling. At times, Ignacio took his anger out on the actors, and invariably, Dominic's scenes took an unreasonably long time to complete. It reached the point where Dominic couldn't utter a single line of dialogue without making some gaff.

One day, when they broke for lunch, Dominic decided to get away from everyone for a while. He walked past the catering van and discreetly exited through the metal barriers. What started as a brisk walk to help burn off some of his frustration turned into a lengthy sightseeing trek across the city. The busy streets of Montevideo offered welcome refuge from the tensions on the set. His eyes and ears absorbed every tiny detail as he navigated his way around the main roads. With the "Gateway of The Citadel" on one side and the start of 18 de Julio Avenue on the other, this part of Montevideo was the city's commercial hub. Dominic stopped to admire the country's oldest theater, Solis Theatre. Then he took a quick look at Palacio Salvo, a twenty-six-story building completed in the 1920s that was once the tallest building in Uruguay. He also saw Estevez Palace and the Executive Tower, the President of Uruguay's workplaces. He knew he didn't have time to go inside the buildings or stop and examine the exteriors for more than a few minutes. It didn't really matter. A short, casual look was enough—for now. At some point later, he planned to wander around the city, looking at the sights in more detail. He had been told that Ignacio rarely filmed on Sundays, so he decided that this coming Sunday morning, he would saunter along Tristán Narvaja Street, trying to blend in with the locals, observing the vendors at La Feria Tristán Narvaja Flea Market sell anything and everything from t-shirts and kitchen supplies to antiques and puppies. On Sunday evening, he hoped to walk along the Rambia—a waterside roadway—and at sunset, he would sit and drink *mate*, idly watching people fish and bicycle past and then stare at the picturesque waterfront views until long after dark.

After a while, he sat on a bench and took off his right shoe. He could feel blisters forming near the big toe and the heel. While he massaged his foot, the sun glinted off the clock face of his Omega Quartz watch, and he became aware of the time, realizing he had been away from the set for over an hour. The day's filming was terrible enough without him adding to the problems. He put his shoe on and headed back as fast as he could. Unfortunately, the quicker he moved, the more his foot hurt. He winced through the discomfort, knowing he had more to worry about than blistered feet.

He located the catering van and slithered between the temporary metal gates once again, moving them back in place once he was on the right side of them. Then, as quickly and discreetly as possible, he scurried back to where the film crew had set up their equipment, unaware that Ignacio had caught sight of him.

"Dominic!" Ignacio called out.

At the same moment, Dominic barged past one of the extras, apologizing as he did so. He failed to hear Ignacio, and when he reached his seat, believing he had made it back unobserved, he grabbed the newspaper that hung over the arm of the chair, opened it up so that it masked his face, and pretended to read. Dominic became aware of Ignacio's presence when four fingers appeared over the top of his page, pulling the newspaper away from him.

Ignacio stared at him with annoyance. "We've been looking

everywhere for you. You've been gone for ages."

Dominic struggled to find an excuse to explain his absence, and when he eventually opened his mouth to speak, Ignacio interrupted him, saying, "There's been a small change in the script." He shoved some crumpled pages into Dominic's hand. "I'm sure you can learn the new lines very quickly."

"What's changed?" asked Dominic cynically, quickly scanning the revised scene.

"The scene needed something extra."

"I see you've added Sofía to the scene," said Dominic, visibly irked.

He also noticed that his dialogue had been trimmed. Sofía now had the same number of lines as him. He looked up at Ignacio and said dourly, "Did Sofía suggest these changes?"

"She did," admitted Ignacio. "And she was right to suggest them. The scene needs her."

Dominic's lips tightened. He crumpled the paper in his fist and said, "I preferred the earlier version."

"References to Officer Sanchez make later scenes clearer," defended Ignacio. "We might even be able to eliminate the scene between you and the call girl."

"Can we try both versions?" he implored, downhearted that Ignacio intended to cut one of his better scenes.

Ignacio gave him a weary smile. "No time. We're battling against the clock."

He walked away before Dominic could protest further.

———— ✦ ————

Later that day, as two loudmouthed, burly men wrestled him to the ground with unnecessary force, he tried not to scream out in terror. The sight of Luis wielding a large, heavy axe was almost too much to bear. He was sure the careless oaf would bring the blade down on his neck instead of his arm. He wanted to shut his eyes and grit his teeth, but he knew Ignacio would make them do the scene over, so he watched, in abject terror, gabbling his nonsense dialogue as the blade came down, severing his imitation limb.

He screeched so violently that the two men pinning him to the ground squirmed free of him. Though impromptu, it was nevertheless effective as far as the director was concerned.

Dominic stared in alarm at the latex arm, now detached from his torso. He was pale and nauseous, awash with panic, looking fixedly at the blood spurting out of his body. The grisly effect, best suited to a horror flick, was traumatizing.

"Cut!" said Ignacio, elated. "Print it."

Dominic let out a feeble moan and tried not to let others see that he was visibly shaking. The props were lethal, the stunts unnecessarily dangerous. The director seemed to delight in terrorizing his actors.

Dominic closed his eyes and tried to control his breathing. His stress level was way too high. He needed a two-month supply of Valium and an on-call masseuse. He didn't know how to make it through the day, let alone the entire shoot. The fiend behind this lurid charade needed locking up in a padded cell. *Someone should swing that horrible axe at his head*, thought Dominic hatefully.

Sixteen

ONE evening, while Dominic was trying to steal some much-needed sleep, the telephone on the bedside table stirred him awake. The actor grabbed the receiver, holding it slightly away from his ear, fretful that Maria Romero was about to bark some vitriolic comment. The prospect of returning to the film set extra early to cram in extra scenes was depressing.

The silky-smooth voice on the line surprised him.

"Dominic Graves? The actor?"

The stranger's crisp, enunciated words were pleasant and laudable. His voice was American, pure Californian. Oddly, his distinctive brogue had a familiar ring.

"Yes, this is Dominic Graves. Do I know you?"

"Don't think we've met. My name's Jay Adler-Frankel."

The receiver felt like it wanted to leap out of Dominic's hand. "Jay Adler-Frankel? The actor?"

"Yep, that's the one. Although my wife might disagree. I don't happen upon that much work these days."

Dominic sat up in bed, startled into full, wild-eyed consciousness. "Christ! What the heck's going on? This must be a dream."

"Jules Fern gave me your number. I met her at a conference at the weekend. She mentioned you were doing that God-awful movie in Uruguay. Bullet in the Brain."

"A Bullet for Silver Face."

"Ah, yes, that's the one."

"This is incredible. I can't believe I'm getting a call from Jay Adler-Frankel."

"How funny. Jules said you would say that. It's as if she scripted it."

"Smart girl, Jules," Dominic murmured. "I'm predictable, and boy does she know it. How come you're phoning me?"

"Jules thought it might be useful for us to chat. Maybe she's hoping I'll give you character insight for the movie."

"That sounds useful. Can you?"

"'Fraid I can't help you there," admitted Jay. "My perspective on the character wouldn't benefit you much anyway. What the hell do I know about anything? To tell the truth, I didn't like the script much. The character didn't have a lot of complexity."

"Think I share your opinions about the script," sighed Dominic.

"Best advice I can give is to walk away."

Dominic scratched his head and stared at the wall. His room felt less like a luxury chamber and more like solitary confinement. "Walk away," he muttered dismally.

"Quit while you still have your health, Dominic. That director is the biggest real-life villain you'll ever meet. The moment you step in front of the camera, you'll regret ever going to Uruguay."

"Oops," said Jay. "Now I'm embarrassed. Didn't realize."

"Maybe it's not too late to walk," Dominic murmured aloud. "What happened to *you*? You were supposed to be the lead. Did *you* walk?"

"Well, I was about to, but I didn't get the chance. Had a bit of an accident with one of the director's cars. Not my finest hour."

"Crashed a Porsche 968 Turbo RS, I heard."

"Don't remind me.

"Ignacio Martinez couldn't have been too happy about it."

"He was livid. The spiteful ogre tried to murder me."

"Not all that surprising, though, is it?"

"A little over-the-top, don't you think? I didn't expect to be running for my life."

"What? I'm confused. What do you mean?"

"The sonofabitch ordered a hit on me."

"A hit?"

"A mob hit. What else?"

Dominic shook his head. His fellow actor was clearly bonkers. "You make him sound like a gangster."

"Coz he is. Didn't you know? He's deeply involved with organized crime groups. Everything from arms and drug and human trafficking. Money laundering and counterfeiting, as well, I imagine. He's part of a gang that controls Villa Española, Peñarol, and a few other neighborhoods. A real bad hombre. Gave the order to his Mafioso clan to bury me alive within hours of my crash. He didn't care if I was injured; he just wanted vengeance because I put a crinkle in his precious sports car."

"A crinkle. That the damage? I thought you mangled it beyond repair. My agent made it sound like you slammed into the wall of a building at full speed."

"Your agent is full of crap. Bernie Finkelman, isn't it?"

"That's right."

"He's the biggest liar in LA. A total jerk. He has a serpent's tongue and claws for fingers."

"I see you've met him. I couldn't have described him any better."

"He's half right about the Porsche, though," Jay conceded. "The car did hit a wall, and my speed was certainly up there in the high digits. But damn, those cars are built for speed and reinforced like tanks, aren't they? A panel beater could have got it back in shape. I hardly *totaled* it!"

Dominic was silent, not quite sure how to respond. It was hard to know what to believe, but Jay's version sounded like a cock and bull story.

"Didn't they take you to hospital?"

"Ignacio wouldn't hear of it. He wanted to open me up with

a pair of pliers and remove my vital organs, not pack me off to hospital to recuperate."

"Then where the heck did you go?"

"I ran off down the street, Dominic. Ran for my life. That's what I'm trying to tell you. If it wasn't for my agent, I wouldn't be alive. He had me picked up ten minutes later and driven to a private airfield. Got me a chartered flight out of there before Ignacio's thugs could catch up to me."

"That's quite the story," marveled Dominic, thinking it sounded better than the plot to *A Bullet for Silver Face*.

"Real gallant man, my agent. Ted Ferro. You should look him up. He's not like the Bernie Finkelmans of this world. That douchebag wouldn't lift a finger to save anyone. He's not got your back, Dominic. Hood like that would sooner put a knife in it."

Dominic didn't doubt it. He cupped the telephone receiver against his ear with his shoulder and grabbed a pen off the bedside table. "Ted Ferro, you said? That two rrs?"

"Yep."

Dominic jotted down the name, intending to call the agent immediately.

"Ditch the picture the first chance you get, Dominic," insisted Jay. "That hood will land you in a body bag."

Dominic thanked him wholeheartedly, fully committed to finding a way back home at first light. Bernie was adamant that the film would open doors for Dominic, so quitting the picture wouldn't help his career. But it would sure as hell give his mind and soul a much-needed boost.

"South America beckons," Bernie had told him, thumping his desk with malice to emphasize the point. "Provided you give the acting performance of your life."

Dominic's rough weeks in Uruguay encouraged him to exit the country while he still could. With luck, Ted Ferro would put Dominic on his books and find the actor promising parts closer to home.

Moments after he returned the receiver to its cradle, the shrill chime of the telephone sounded once more. He answered the call, thinking Jay was calling him back, and was surprised to hear Maria Romero on the line. Her voice was loud and sharp.

"You're needed on the set, Dominic," she told him, barking the order at him. "Pronto!"

———— ✦ ————

When Dominic arrived on the set, he was ushered into a boutique store, which was used as a temporary waiting room for the actors and crewmembers. The people gathered inside were fidgeting impatiently, jostling for an extra inch of carpet area. Personal space was a much sought-after commodity.

Dominic nudged his way into the claustrophobic room. Though eager to get back outside, the sizable gathering indicated that something important had gone down, and he was curious to know exactly what had happened.

All heads were turned to Sebastián Pereira. He was leading a lively discussion and looking cheerier than ever. Few people had paid much attention to the man before now, so it was strange to watch him commandeer an audience.

As Dominic moved between the crowd, craning to get a better look, he heard someone ask, "But who's in charge?"

Sebastián's eyes twinkled with jubilation. "*I* am. I'm taking over things starting this morning."

It was an alarming announcement—or rather, Dominic found it alarming.

"Is that the studio's decision or yours?"

"The studio."

"Is it permanent or temporary? Will a new director be appointed?"

Sebastián smiled happily. He was enjoying his moment in the limelight, relishing being the center of attention for once. "It's still being discussed, but they want me to finish the movie."

"Christ!" someone muttered.

The remark echoed Dominic's sentiments. He could scarcely believe what he was hearing. Nobody had relayed any news to him when he had stepped out of his taxi that morning, anticipating a normal day at work.

As his workday had never been anything verging on ordinary, this new announcement shouldn't have come as a great surprise. It was yet another squall of drama. Somehow, despite the constant wave of setbacks, the film hadn't sunk. Not yet.

The adverse reaction to Sebastián's appointment didn't faze the man. He kept on smiling, radiating dazzling self-assurance. "It's been a strange start to the day," he said matter-of-factly. "Truth is, I'm as surprised as you all are."

"Did Ignacio quit?" asked Dominic, unable to keep his thoughts to himself.

Sebastián gave him a reproving look. He was irked that he had to explain it all again.

"He left by mutual consent. Out of left field, I know. He was walked off the set early today."

Standing directly in front of Dominic, Luis turned to the actor and said in a low, confiding voice, "Ignacio was asked to leave by the studio."

"Sacked?"

"Yes, sacked," clarified Luis. "And dragged off the film set."

The revelation startled Dominic. It shouldn't have, though. It had been on the cards from the moment Dominic set foot in Montevideo. The director had been a menace. His decisions were insane, and his lack of concern for his actors and crew was despicable. That wasn't the tipping point, of course. Money had made the difference. It was his lack of regard for the budget that toppled him.

"The studio is going to close down the picture, aren't they?" said Sofía, pessimistically.

"Not at all," insisted Sebastián. "I won't let that happen. Let's deal with the next phase like nothing has happened."

"What a thing to say. How can we?" argued Sofía.

"We can save this picture, can't we?" Sebastián hotly responded. "If we all throw ourselves into our work, we can make the movie Ignacio wanted. Maybe we can make a better movie than he imagined."

"We have to start from scratch."

Sebastián shook his head. "We'll edit what's already been shot and make it work. No point reinventing the wheel."

"What's he on about?" Luis muttered.

Something was lost in translation. Dominic didn't bother to explain.

"Our equipment's working. We know what remaining scenes we must shoot. Everyone is on board, so there's nothing to stop us from wrapping this picture up on time and doing it well."

"I'm all for that," said Dominic, almost shouting the words.

Buoyed that Ignacio was finally out of his hair, he felt exhilarated and keen to get to work. Though he thought the Assistant Director was an irritating oaf, he knew the importance of giving the man full support. It was beastly toadying, the kind he typically looked down on, but today, it felt like the appropriate thing to do.

Sofía glowered at Dominic. "This is Ignacio's film. He's the reason we're all here. It doesn't feel right to do this movie without him."

"He'd want me to finish it for him," pressed Sebastián. "To do it *his* way."

"We might even finish it three times faster," added the cameraman.

The timidity was gone from him. He looked proud and confident, like a man reborn. Although his arm was still in a cast, he twitched with energy and keenness, looking like he wanted to punch the air with his bad arm.

"Yes, yes," smiled Sebastián. "We finish this ahead of schedule and think what it will say about us."

He was clearly thinking of his own career and desperate to make a good impression with the powers that be. The excitement in his eyes was borderline obscene.

Sebastián's optimism lifted the spirits of some of those around him. Whether or not he could salvage the movie remained to be seen, but the overriding mood was positive rather than negative.

"If filming falls further behind schedule, it's a clear invitation to shelve the picture, isn't it?" observed a technician.

The candid remark drew murmurs of agreement.

Though unhappy about Ignacio's dismissal, Sofía conceded that she didn't want the production to halt. It was her most prominent role to date, and she had high hopes that the movie would earn her glowing reviews and help establish her as an international star.

"We're making a good movie, don't you think?" she said aloud, scrutinizing the faces of those around her.

"I think what we're doing is marvelous," lied Dominic.

Other crew members spoke up, voicing their commitment to the project. Remarkably, support for Sebastián proved strong indeed.

"What are we shooting today?" asked Dominic, having forgotten to look at his call sheet.

Sebastián gave an involuntary shudder, wishing Dominic's choice of words had been more delicately chosen.

Seventeen

A WEEK passed, and it all felt like a blur of frenetic activity. There were lots of costume and location changes. There was not much sitting around; it was just action, action, action.

Dominic kicked off his shoes and sat on the bed in his hotel room, thoroughly exhausted. His body throbbed, and the pain behind his eyes was insufferable. The charmless Sebastián Pereira had proved himself to be a hard taskmaster. He was obsessed with hurrying things along, devoid of perfectionism. There was no idling, no artistic flair. As long as the words matched what was in the script and nobody made any gaffes, he was happy with the end product. A scene didn't often need a second take.

Unfortunately, Sebastián's tetchiness and continual whining when things weren't going so well made Dominic want to rescind his support for the man. Sebastián was consumed with packing a day's filming with bonus shots and tomorrow's scenes. He didn't like actors messing up his rhythm, and he didn't want to stop, not even when filming was supposed to be done for the day.

Dominic began to wonder if he had judged Ignacio too harshly. He wasn't convinced he could honestly say that Sebastián was an improvement on the last director. Both men were exasperating in their own distinctive way.

Dominic rested one leg over the other and took off his sock. The foot was slightly swollen, and the heel ached terribly. He massaged the foot, feeling the blisters that had formed on the mound of his big toe and the outer heel with his fingers. The one consolation was that they were one giant leap closer to finishing the picture. The week might almost have been a success…if it weren't for the niggling fear that *A Bullet for Silver Face* may be worse than he imagined. Without Ignacio at the helm, would it actually get a theatrical release?

Dominic stopped massaging his foot and set it down on the floor. His other foot hurt almost as much. He rested that leg over his knee and took off the sock. Though not swollen, there were multiple blisters, this time around the neck of his big toe, the fourth toe mound, and on the edge of the little toe. There was also a blister on the bottom of his outer ankle. They were such tiny blemishes, but they hurt like hell.

He gently rubbed his foot for a few minutes, managing to ease the pain somewhat, and when he eased himself down onto his back, he thought pensively about Ignacio's dismissal. Frequently prickly, aggressive, and argumentative, the man could be as irritating as the blisters on Dominic's feet. And he was reckless to the point of madness. His views on live ammunition and putting loaded weapons in his actor's hands made him the last man on earth you would want to see directing people. A man like that might be more at home in an asylum than on a movie set.

Remarkably, he hadn't shown signs of lunacy when Dominic had dined with him a few days earlier. In fact, Ignacio had come across as quite charming. He certainly knew a thing or two about fine dining, and as far as good manners and table etiquette went, Ignacio was a gentleman. Pity he was also a brute. Possibly even a gangster.

Dominic put his hands behind his head and let his eyes drift across the patterned ceiling. Óscar Chiosso was no saint, either. He didn't have a good word to say about anybody, least of all Ignacio, and was prone to getting under people's skin. Plainly, he was a loudmouth with a talent for antagonizing people. Chiosso must have worked tirelessly to get him fired.

What was next for Ignacio? Though this might not have marked the end of his career, it was quite possibly on the downswing.

Dominic's eyes wandered across the room, settling on the refrigerator. It seemed like a good time to work his way through the minibar.

He rolled off the bed and got back on his feet. It was an appropriate hour for tequila, he decided. *Or was he in the mood for rum?* He started toward the fridge but didn't make it all the way. He wished to God he hadn't had to give up his hotel suite. He missed the four-poster bed and the Jacuzzi. But, most of all, he missed the drinks cabinet.

To hell with the minibar! Drinking expensive miniatures alone in a shoebox room took a vital ingredient out of the drinking experience. He figured he would have more fun in the bar downstairs.

He put his socks and shoes back on and limped out of his room and into the elevator. He thought a few drinks would help him unwind. In hindsight, he should have stuck to the minibar.

It was busy in the restaurant, and the bar area was packed with an interesting blend of people who seemed to have surfaced from all parts of the globe, judging by their clothes and physical composition. Naturally enough, all the seats around the counter were taken, and small clusters of people hovered behind the seated patrons, cradling drinks and talking loudly to one another in varied foreign tongues. The boisterous din and swarm of bodies might otherwise have discouraged Dominic from wanting to battle his way to the bar to get the same drink he could enjoy in the solitude of his comfortable hotel room, but he was eager for distractions. Right then, anything seemed better than sitting alone on his bed, staring at the walls. Besides, his throat was too parched to care much about anything besides getting fluid down it, and water wasn't the liquid he had in mind. Seeing all these people quaffing colorful cocktails and appealing-looking wines made him all the thirstier. He didn't think twice about brusquely jostling people out of his way, muttering insincere apologies as he worked his way determinedly to the bar. He reached the counter remarkably quickly, and, after elbowing some room for himself, he raised a hand and muttered a few words of greeting to the barman, part out of politeness but mostly to let the man know he was waiting to be served.

The barman wasn't much of a talker. His impassive eyes caught sight of Dominic, and his eyebrows quivered ever so faintly. Dominic's previous interactions informed him that this was the man's way of asking what he wanted to drink. He pointed to a bottle of Mac Pay whisky. The barman seemed to nod, although it was hard to tell. He then slowly served two other people, making Dominic wonder if a drop of liquor would ever make it to his lips. His thoughts wandered to the last time he had stood at the bar and ordered a drink. *Had he given an adequate tip?* Actually, he couldn't recall having tipped at all.

"*Whisky, por favor.*"

Having heard his accent, the woman to his immediate left instantly turned around. "Dominic," she said with a smile, touching his arm.

For a fraction of a second, he didn't recognize Sofía. She was dressed elegantly in a low-cut outfit, her hair tied up in a prim bun, pretty ornaments about her ears, and a sparkling necklace distracting the onlooker's eye from her conspicuous cleavage. She was naturally striking, with an air of sophistication and expensive tastes. His eyes finally ceased probing her clothes and accessories for long enough to appreciate her face. She had overdone the foundation and powder to the extent that it was a cake-face. Nevertheless, she looked about five years younger.

"Come and join us," she said, patting his hand delicately.

He peered past her and recognized crew members from earlier in the day.

Luis got off his stool and said, "Dominic, you can sit here." He slapped the seat cushion so hard that a small puff of dust sprang up, then turned to the barman and clicked his fingers. "*Necesitamos otro taburete.*"

A moment later, a stool was hoisted over the counter and set down next to Sofía. The others made room for the American actor.

Dominic thanked Luis, humbled by the man's courteousness. During his first weeks in Uruguay, he hadn't interacted much with the other actors, mistakenly under the impression that they disliked him. He now regretted having been so aloof.

Sofía put a hand on his shoulder when he sat down on the stool. "What are you drinking?"

"Whiskey."

She turned to the barman to place the order, but before she could utter a word, he set a glass down on the counter in front of Dominic. Dominic was quick to reach for it.

"I'm not surprised to see you in the bar," said Sofía. "I think after a day like today, we could all use a drink."

Sebastián leaned over, saying, "But not so many that you don't make it to the set on time."

"No need to worry. I'll be on time," vowed Dominic. "Even if it means staying up all night in this bar to make sure I don't oversleep."

Although others laughed, Sebastián fought to keep a smile on his face. Now, head honcho, he was wary of colleagues undermining his authority.

"Everyone, let us toast the fantastic new director," said Sofía, beaming at him.

"Yes, yes," agreed Luis, the first to lift his glass. "*A tiempos mejores.*"

"To better times," she translated.

As they each rattled their glasses, Sebastián seemed slightly embarrassed by their generous encouragement.

"I am sorry I was too energetic in our scenes," Luis said earnestly.

Dominic shrugged. "It was nothing. Forget about it."

"No, no," insisted Luis. "I was too rough. I hit you hard."

"Didn't feel it."

"I slugged you, and it wasn't professional. Ignacio kept telling me to make our fights look real, and I took him at his word. It was too physical, don't you think? The pushing and kicking and the wrestling for the gun…I didn't like it."

"Can't say I liked it either," said Dominic.

"When you threw up, I thought I had cracked your ribs, maybe damaged your organs."

"It was my stomach," confided Dominic. "It was full of booze."

"You drink between scenes?" Luis asked suspiciously. In fact, he looked rather appalled.

Dominic glanced at Sebastián. He was fearful the man had overheard. Fortunately, the director was talking to Sofía, practically chewing her ear off.

"I don't usually drink on the set," Dominic explained. "The hairstylist plied me with liquor. She seemed to think it would cure my headache."

Luis nodded with understanding, although his face was full of alarm. His eyes gravitated to the drink in Dominic's hand. The sight of the whiskey didn't improve the mood.

"Bottom's up," said Dominic, draining his glass.

The supporting actor's lips tightened as Dominic poured the whiskey down his throat like water. Dominic had emptied his glass a little too speedily, sending a clear message to his fellow actor that he was a man with a problem and, more than likely, a man who would cause problems.

Luis' reproving stare made him want to wriggle free. He set the empty glass down on the bar and turned toward Sofía. Unfortunately, she offered no comfort—far from it. Her sycophantic manner irritated him, and he stared at her with sourness. The way she was behaving around Sebastián was nauseating. He understood where it would lead and was more than a little jealous.

Unwisely, he dropped his hand in her lap, squeezing her thigh. Her intimate bond with Ignacio had made him want to be rid of her for the sake of their careers. Now that Ignacio was off the picture, there was no reason why he shouldn't allow their passion for one another to run wild.

Sadly, the action didn't have the desired effect. Her body tensed, and though she deliberately avoided eye contact with him, her face was pinched, her smile evaporating fast. If anything, there was panic in her eyes. She was fixated on Sebastián, nodding at everything he said, and the fact that she was ignoring Dominic entirely made his self-worth wither as swiftly as plucked wildflower.

Discreetly, she pried Dominic's hand from her body and shoved it aside with callousness. It made him scowl and want to cause a scene. It was galling that she was fawning over Sebastián and not him.

He pressed his hand against the small of her back, knowing it would aggravate her. Then he leaned in close and murmured bawdy remarks in her ear, enjoying the sound of his voice. She turned and looked at him. She had a smile on her face, but it was joyless, loveless, and tinged with distaste.

"You look tired," she told him, her cautionary stare giving him fiery signals.

"I'm fine."

"Desperately tired," she continued. "Like old age has crept up on you."

The catty observation stabbed him in the chest. He recovered quickly and responded without a telling pause, "You say the sweetest things, darling."

"You should go to bed. You'll never wake up on time otherwise."

"How sweet. I like that you're always looking out for me."

"Goodnight."

She turned and picked up her conversation with Sebastián as if nothing had happened.

Dominic excused himself and trudged away, regretting having gone to the bar. He stepped into the elevator feeling odious and unsightly. The agony in the pit of his stomach was worse than indigestion.

"Damn!" he muttered under his breath.

He jabbed his finger hard against the button to close the doors. Then, just as aggressively, he poked the button to take him to the second floor. As the doors closed and he began his ascent, he cast away any warmth he felt for Sofía. Her egomania was of epic proportions, yet her acting faculties were infinitesimal.

Dominic knew the jury was still out on whether he was a worthy leading man. Unfortunately, while *A Bullet for Silverface* was his best hope of establishing a bonafide career beyond the B-movie rank, the low-grade script didn't offer much encouragement. Ignacio Martinez had been the natural star attraction, and now that he had been sacked, the project felt like it had become a C-movie. Dominic's chances of finding his way to a speaking role in a Hollywood movie had taken another blow, and the worrisome impulse plaguing his thoughts was that his baloney performance might crown him the year's biggest turd actor in a foreign picture.

Right then, he had no inkling of the sizable impact this little production would have on the movie world. Had he known what was in store, and the stress he would have to endure, he would have thrown himself down the elevator shaft.

CHANGEOVER

MONTEVIDEO, URUGUAY
FEBRUARY 1997

Eighteen

THE production bounced along like a racecar speeding around an open-pit mine, with Dominic doing his best to keep up with the director. Locales changed every few days, set-ups doubled, and he had pages of unwieldy dialogue to memorize. Mornings were long, punishing affairs with barely a pause between takes. Afternoons stretched into the evening, and nobody dared to complain, concerned about impeding his creative zeal and waylaying the production.

The absence of script changes was a small blessing. Dominic had managed to learn by heart his tawdry lines. Nothing his character said was moving or memorable. Bruce Pucker seemed to be the most insipid and unenlightened journalist the world had ever known.

The moment filming was done for the day, Dominic habitually hit the bars in town, quaffing booze with infinite gluttony. There wasn't a night that passed that he didn't fall asleep with a shot glass in his hand. Regrettably, the alcohol-inflicted pounding sensation in his head, marring each of his mornings, reached the point where he could scarcely function. Despite feeling ghastly, he somehow made it to work, determined to complete his scenes. His sluggishness was evident to everyone, and his sickly pallor suggested he would benefit from a day in bed, but he kept telling himself that the competent crew knew how to make him appear ten times better on screen than he really looked in person. He could be made to look like a Greek Adonis with the proper lighting, some imaginative camerawork, and the makeup artist on hand to cover up any conspicuous blemishes on his skin.

When he stopped in front of Sebastián, shafts of sunlight stalking his bloodshot eyes, the director examined him circumspectly, perturbed by what he saw. Dominic's pores oozed the sickly sweet scent of hard liquor, and his tired eyes radiated a powerful glimmer of rakishness.

"You look ghoulish. Worse than I've ever seen you. Are you well enough to perform?" Sebastián asked.

"I feel great," Dominic said, pushing out his chest, though the blinding pain behind his eyes prevented him from holding Sebastián's gaze.

The director's lips were fixed in a grim expression, looking like he had just experienced a strong and unpleasant whiff of feces. "Dominic, your face is drawn, and all the color has drained from your cheeks. And just look at those eyes! Hell, they are *hideously* bloodshot. The special effects department couldn't make you look more grotesque."

Dominic shrugged. "Maybe I stared at the sun too long. As for my body, right now, I could run a mile in under six minutes."

With a shake of his head, Sebastián said, "Either you over-exerted yourself practicing your lines, or you have been nursing a bottle of whiskey all morning. I think maybe you should get some sleep. Perhaps also some breakfast. You're haggard. When was the last time you ate a meal?" He noticed Dominic's grimace, making him add, "You look gaunter every day. It's like you have stopped eating altogether. Not a good idea, Dominic. You're going to need the extra energy. Later this morning, you'll have to chase Miguel through the street and tackle him to the ground. Are you sure you have the stamina for such a scene?"

"Of course," said Dominic, sounding mildly offended.

"In the afternoon, there is a torture scene in the train depot."

"You don't need to remind me."

"Your hands and feet will be trussed up with an electric cord. Seven police officers will kick and punch every part of your convulsing body for five minutes until you're a gory pulp. Then, what remains of your face will be hacked open with a carving knife, and salt poured into the wounds."

Dominic shuddered at the graphic description of what lay in store for his character. He was under the impression that the life of a newspaper journalist was dreary and unremarkable. Not in Uruguay, apparently.

"You had better go to Suzette, our special effects makeup artist. You'll need to sit in a chair for several hours, getting your makeup applied. It will be tiring," Sebastián warned, eyeing him solemnly.

"I'll survive," said Dominic evenly.

Sebastián looked him up and down and said sternly, "Get yourself something to eat, Dominic."

Dominic's stomach chose that moment to give a low growl. Though faint, it was loud enough for Sebastián to hear.

"There. I'm right," Sebastián said arrogantly. "Your stomach is speaking to you. It's literally crying out for food."

He shooed Dominic away with a slight air of disdain.

Dominic chided himself, wishing he had shown a little restraint the night before. While he trudged away, the image of his decrepit agent popped into his head. He pictured the man at his desk, waving his cane about and calling Dominic a fool. Naturally, the ornery old man would offer some cutting remark about Dominic's lack of restraint in the drinking department— something derogatory that would make Dominic feel as appealing as discovering a dead frog in a bowl of tapioca pudding.

"You can drown yourself in a vat of whiskey for all I care," Bernie would likely grumble, "but just wait a while, can't you? Dig your feet in and get the film made for the sake of the contract. Hold out for the residuals."

Bile came up in Dominic's throat as he recalled some of the

rancid things his agent had said to him over the years. Bernie was a vile creature, prone to inexcusable outbursts. Tooth extraction was more pleasurable than an appointment with him.

As the wind picked up, quivering the palm trees, the rustle of fronds in the warm breeze made Dominic give an anxious glance over his shoulder. The curving shadows seemed to stalk his movements, and he thought he could hear the low murmur of a voice. He half-expected to find Bernie trailing behind him, dirtying the air with his foul language. Mercifully, no one was within spitting distance, but he quickened his pace nonetheless.

———— ✦ ————

The special effects makeup artist had an extraordinary talent for dialogue. Hours slid by, yet barely a minute passed without her gassing about something. Dominic sat helplessly in his chair, trapped in her claustrophobic compartment, unable to do anything but grunt in agreement and wish he was somewhere else. Eventually, she allowed him to get up and leave, and as he stepped outside, overjoyed by a snatched moment of solitude, he spotted Sebastián and felt his heart rate accelerate. The sight of the director was a reminder of the potentially bruising scene they were about to shoot. He didn't like the idea of rolling around on the ground, feigning pain, while half a dozen burly extras pretended to kick him. It felt like a recipe for disaster.

While Dominic sat in Suzette's chair, letting her apply his makeup, he tried to focus on something other than her inane chatter. He had silently rehearsed his lines for the subsequent scene and found he wasn't happy with the words. Typically, once the camera was rolling, all the elements of his performance came together. He liked to think he was an actor who worked best under pressure—provided he wasn't in mortal danger. His idea of pressure was more along the lines of live television than having fellow actors shoot at him with real bullets. A live audience was usually enough to bring out the best in his acting, while the latter seemed more like a live execution. On this occasion, he figured it was worth addressing his qualms about the dialogue in the scene, particularly as Sebastián appeared to have a moment to spare. Flapping the pages of his script at Sebastián, he asked, "Can we talk about the script?"

Sebastián glanced at him for a split second, riveted by the actor's macabre makeup. Dominic's grotesque appearance pleased him. His smile was fleeting, and his patience evaporated seconds later. "No," he finally muttered testily. "Not now."

Dominic thumbed the pages of his script, trying to find a specific section, unmindful of Sebastián's hostile face.

"I don't like these lines," he moaned without looking up from the page. "If I speak the dialogue the way it's written, it will sound like English is my second language. I'm supposed to be a journalist for *USA Today*." He ran his finger across the page, silently reading the sentences to verify that it was the correct passage. "Yes, it's no good," he concluded, sure of himself now. "Take a look."

He held the script up to the director, tapping at the bottom half of the page. "Okay, so after Aguero pushes Pucker onto the hood of the car and tells him to go home, I say—"

"Can't this wait until later?" Sebastián said, swatting the script away.

"Here, I'll read the lines to you."

Sebastián groaned inwardly as Dominic began to read his part. The way the actor emphasized the poorly constructed fragments of dialogue was excruciating, and Sebastián stared at him with mounting impatience, desperate for the ordeal to be over.

"Well?" said Dominic, finally completing his monologue.

"Well, what?" snapped Sebastián.

"It's garbage, isn't it? My nine-year-old nephew has a superior grasp of the rudiments of English grammar. It's wordy, clumsy, and witless, and I don't like it one iota. It doesn't reflect my character, either. Pucker is too smart to deliver this sort of gibberish."

He waited for feedback, but Sebastián was curiously silent. His pained look persuaded Dominic to try a different tactic.

"I have some ideas for improving the language. How about I rewrite the lines how I think they should be said? Let me give you an example."

"How about you keep it to yourself?" muttered Sebastián.

Dominic seemed not to hear him, and having cleared his throat, he recited his scene again. His delivery was more cogent, but Sebastián's aggrieved expression remained.

Eventually, wearying of Dominic's turgid monologue, the director brusquely cut him off. "Do what you think is best."

Dominic blinked at him, wondering if he had misheard the director.

"Other actors have hounded me this past week with complaints about the script," Sebastián admitted. "One demanded a rewrite, and another proposed additional monologues. Someone even handed me supplementary scenes. The scriptwriter is desperately keen to wring the neck of the next person who voices objections."

Dominic frowned. "I hardly think the writer will take umbrage if I improve his script. I imagine he'll thank me."

"It's your call," said Sebastián diplomatically.

"You mean you don't care?"

"What I mean is that I don't mind."

Dominic's frown lingered. "There are some other lines of dialogue I'd like to go over with you."

He leafed through the script, and as he did so, Sebastián moved to leave.

"Just a moment," urged Dominic. "Let me find the page."

Sensing that Sebastián was rapidly losing interest, he frantically flipped through the pages, annoyed that he hadn't highlighted the cumbrous sentences in ink.

"I have got to go," said Sebastián, attempting to move past Dominic.

The actor blocked him. "It won't take a moment, I promise."

Sebastián curled his lip in irritation. He wanted to grab the script and see how far he could throw it.

Dominic soon found the pertinent section and angled the script so Sebastián could see the passage. Sebastián's shoulders sagged as the actor traced the line with his finger. "It goes: Why would you tell me—"

Sebastián placed his hand over the page, halting Dominic mid-sentence. "You do what you think best."

Dominic was delighted by the suggestion. "I'll just tweak the sentences a little bit to make them sound more natural."

"Knock yourself out."

"How will the writer react? He won't stoop to anything stupid, will he? I wouldn't want him to retaliate."

Sebastián shrugged indifferently. "He's not what you would call a good-natured type, but I'm sure he won't stick a knife in your back. He did serve time in prison once, but that was long ago."

Dominic's eyes filled with apprehension. "What was his crime? Tax evasion?" he asked hopefully.

"GBH, I think," Sebastián replied. "But as I said, that was long ago, and he's atoned for his sins. I hear he's thick-skinned now and almost impervious to criticism."

The optimism had extinguished from Dominic's eyes.

"Anyway, I'm not really the go-to person for this," Sebastián confessed guiltily. Script changes require the director's blessing."

"But isn't that you?"

"Not anymore," Sebastián conceded mournfully.

"The studio replaced you already?"

Sebastián nodded with manifest bitterness.

He quietly gazed at Sebastián for a moment, considering the implications. Then, after sucking his tooth for a while, he said, "Where's the new director?"

With a jerk of his head, Sebastián steered Dominic's eyes to the tall, thin lunatic not thirty feet away.

"Oh boy," murmured Dominic, staring in disbelief at Ignacio Martinez.

"It's hard to believe he's back, isn't it?" said Sebastián, jadedly. "Ignacio's a powerful man with many influential friends."

"What about the studio? Surely, Chiosso wouldn't let Ignacio take charge of the picture again?"

"The financiers insisted he return."

Dominic took a long, hard look at Ignacio, speculating about his power. Evidently, he held a lot of sway over the studio.

He would have to fathom some coping strategy to get through the remainder of the picture. There were still another four weeks of filming to withstand, and, knowing Ignacio, there was still plenty of drama yet to unfold.

Nineteen

"I KEEP reminding myself how blessed I am to have such a talented film star in my picture," said Ignacio, pumping Dominic's hand with manly vigor. "Every time I see you, you look more handsome and more...what's the right word? Revitalized. Is that what I mean? I don't really know. I'm sure there's a better word, but this one will do."

The savage strength in Ignacio's thick fingers was evident by the pained look on Dominic's face. The actor had forgotten the ordeal of their very first greeting. The director seemed to delight in crushing people's fingers and pulling on an arm with sufficient force to dislocate shoulders. Dominic tolerated his suffering without complaint, reluctant to concede that he was hurting, but Ignacio didn't let up. His extreme hold persisted, and all the while, his cinnamon-brown eyes bore into Dominic as if trying to gauge how much distress he was inflicting.

Dominic rid his face of emotion, determined to ride out the discomfort and come out on top in the exchange. Alas, Ignacio's grip steadily tightened, and a rush of scorching torment coursed through Dominic's hand until he let out a pathetic moan.

Ignacio quickly apologized, letting go of the actor's hand. "My God, I've hurt you!"

Dominic kneaded his fingers, recoiling from the man. "It's okay, don't worry about it."

"I feel bad. Sometimes, I don't know my own strength."

"Forget about it," said Dominic, smiling bravely. The painful ache in his hand had caused his eyes to water.

"That's the spirit," said Ignacio, jovially slapping his back.

The slap, harder than intended, knocked the breath out of the actor. He staggered numbly and then edged away, fearful of what the director intended to do next.

Ignacio's attention turned to his film crew, watching with contentment as people scuttled around setting up equipment. "It's magnificent to be back at work. I owe everyone an apology. I lost my cool and nearly ruined everything. It's not the first time I've let my emotions get out of hand. I battle to keep my passions in check every day. My heart... How do you say? My heart is on my cuff."

"You wear your heart on your sleeve," corrected Dominic.

"Yes, that's what I meant. It's a nice cliché. Pleasantly poetic." He straightened his neck and put his hands on his hips. "I think today will be a good day, my friend. We've lost three weeks of filming, but we can make up the lost time with hard work."

Dominic found the remark discouraging. Ignacio's approach to getting back on schedule typically meant forcing everyone to work through the night. The idea of shooting fewer takes per scene never occurred to him. "Will Mister Chiosso be joining us today?" he asked.

Ignacio's bottom lip drooped. "Óscar Chiosso won't bother us today."

He pronounced the man's name like it was a dirty word. The assuredness in his declaration was intriguing.

"Is he still connected with the picture?" asked Sebastián.

Ignacio smoothed the hair on his pencil mustache. "He's still attached, but he's concentrating on other projects right now. I assume he's making life difficult for someone else this week."

"All this week?" pressed Sebastián.

Ignacio nodded. "We can get on with things without the burden of Óscar Chiosso for this week at least. With any luck, he won't return at all."

As pleasing as it was to learn that Chiosso might not return, the re-emergence of Ignacio felt as if an unsightly boil had materialized. Dominic's one hope was that the director would try harder to keep his cool. Previously, he had been like touchpaper, with anything liable to set him off. Now that Óscar Chiosso wasn't around, it was conceivable that he might not be quite so volatile.

"Now, about the call sheet," said Ignacio, getting straight to business. "Throw it away. We'll start with scene one-hundred and sixty and then move immediately to scene one-hundred and fifty-one."

"We filmed one-hundred and fifty-one yesterday," Sebastián remarked, believing he was being helpful.

"You didn't capture the right mood. I saw yesterday's rushes and thought, *Jesus Christ, what a disaster*," Ignacio tactlessly stated. "It was a mess. The scene is meant to have humor—not the blunt kind you see in British films. There's no slapstick, asinine faces, farce, or innuendo. I am talking about the subtle kind you find in quality French movies—dry humor that's delivered with a deadpan face."

Dominic nodded pensively. He had yet to discern which lines in the script contained the humor.

"The audience will grin when you say your lines and forgive you for being rude and arrogant in the previous scene."

Having seen some of the rushes, Dominic figured the risible movie would give American audiences much to laugh about. Most of all, they would howl with laughter at his cringe-worthy dialogue and the hammy action moments. It stank as offensively as *Époisses de Bourgogne*.

His mind then wandered back to scene one hundred and fifty-two, a scene that had given him something bordering on satisfaction. In a movie where, all about him, actors were flexing their biceps more than their acting muscles, Dominic felt fortunate to have been allowed to do more than strut and simper in front of the camera. But had his fine work been for naught? Would Ignacio use anything Sebastián had shot?

"Perhaps I could peek at the rest of yesterday's footage," Dominic suggested. "I'm sure there were some interesting takes."

"No," said Ignacio, with conviction. "Sebastián merely added thirty bland minutes to the film. We must reshoot it all."

Ignacio didn't want to let someone else claim a piece of the picture. He was like a cat putting his scent on everything.

"One or two of them weren't bad," Dominic argued. "Sebastián had a good rapport with the other actors. I'd hate for some of my best scenes to end up on the cutting room floor."

"He's not without talent," conceded Ignacio. "But it's important to get the tone right. One inferior scene will spoil the rest of the picture. I have what the scenes should look like in my head." He pointed to where he had set up the camera. "The scene can't be fixed in the editing suite because the camera angles are all wrong. It must be completely reshot. We will do it today. Luckily, we are in the same location."

Dominic groaned inwardly at the thought of reshooting a scene requiring him to chase a live chicken. The hardest part had been when his fellow actor had picked it up and hurled it at him. Dominic could still taste the feathers.

With a cautious glance over his shoulder to make sure nobody was within earshot, Ignacio leaned in close and said to Dominic in a low, confiding tone, "I know what's on your mind."

Dominic flinched and wrinkled his brow. Was his disdain for the director that obvious? "You do?"

"I do," nodded Ignacio, unsmiling. "You think that my approach to the movie is wrong. That Sebastián is better for the picture. He's steady and sensible…uncomplicated. More than that, you like him because he's easy to work with."

While there was some truth to that, Sebastián hadn't been easy to work with, either. They both had their negative points.

"You're wondering if anyone will pay to see the movie," Ignacio continued. "Will it generate adequate video sales to make back its money? Will those who see it hate it? Does it have artistic merit? Why is the director taking so much care with each scene? You believe the script is wanting, and the finished cut can't possibly be any good. Isn't that what you're thinking?"

Though Ignacio had read his mind, wasn't it natural to have those nagging doubts about a movie? Hadn't he felt the same way about previous films?

"Ah, yes," said Ignacio with a knowing smile. "I see I've judged you correctly."

Dominic said indifferently, "Does it matter what I think?"

"Of course it does. The more you care about this movie, the more creative energy you invest in it. That's what I want to see from you—from everyone here, for that matter. We can turn this picture into something exceptional with a little sweat and some TLC. So what if our marketing budget isn't in the millions? That doesn't guarantee anything, anyway. And so what if the picture won't get noticed immediately by the masses and those big mainstream movie critics? A good independent movie is like evergreen or deciduous shrubs. Fast-growing, vibrant, and satisfying. And if the picture doesn't blossom into the sort of thing either of us anticipated, we'll try harder with the next one, won't we?"

"What exactly *are* your expectations?" asked Dominic out of curiosity.

Ignacio glanced about him as if searching for something. His eyes finally settled on the catering van. Then they narrowed in concentration like a man struggling to read a license plate. "I don't exactly know. I have obligations, of course. The studio has financial expectations, and I want to exceed those expectations. I also have personal targets. There are things I value beyond fiscal reward. Twenty years from now, I want to watch this movie with a critical eye and say, *'Now that part I like; that was done well.'* I fully expect to see a scene and think, '*That could have been done better, or that ought to have been done differently.*' What I don't want—the thing I dread most—is that when I watch the movie, a nagging voice inside will yell, *'You surrendered. Ignacio, you took the easy way out and gave up your guns.'* It's one thing to make a mistake, but another thing entirely to be able to correct it and yet do nothing—to deliberately keep an inferior scene in just because you don't want to go through the hassle of a reshoot. If something isn't right and, at the time, I know it isn't right, then I want to have the balls to make it right."

Dominic nodded in agreement.

"And what are *your* expectations?" asked Ignacio.

"I'm still trying to make a name for myself. I've been on the stage and done TV work. I enjoyed both, but I really want to be in movies," explained Dominic. "So far, I've not done one that has given me personal satisfaction. I was desperately hoping this picture might leapfrog me somewhere more fulfilling."

"Somewhere more lucrative?" said Ignacio, rubbing his finger and thumb together.

"I'd love to tell you I do it for the love of acting and not for the money, but I'd be lying. Each piece of acting work is a stepping-stone to the next gig, isn't it? And, naturally, we're all hoping the next gig will have better prospects."

"Sure," said Ignacio, nodding tiredly. "Listen, Dominic. I think you're an actor with limitless potential. That's why I was eager to have you play the lead."

"I hope you don't mind me asking," said Dominic, tentatively, "but I heard a story that Jay Adler-Frankel was contracted to play my part. Apparently, he gave a good reading. Which begs the question: why me and not him?"

Ignacio's facial muscles tightened. He twiddled with his mustache, seemingly disinclined to talk about the man. Then, with a heavy sigh, he recounted the whole story.

"Yes, Jay was my first choice for the role of Bruce Pucker.

He was enthusiastic about the script and eager to do the movie. He gave a good audition. There was an oddball peculiarity to him that I think might have played well into the character. Alas, it was not to be. Despite his keenness, he came across as an imbecile. He broke the chair in my office during one of our meetings. Deliberately, I think. He's quite the eccentric and a danger to himself. In fact, I doubt I will ever meet a man so hell-bent on destruction. He's a ticking bomb, Dominic. One hour after signing the contract to do the movie, he took part in a charity drive through the city. He drove crazily fast through the busy streets and lost control of the gorgeous yellow Porsche 968 Turbo RS he was intentionally abusing—crashed it into the front of a restaurant. He completely destroyed the car and caused damage to the building. And he nearly killed his passenger, an actress friend of mine. How either of them survived the crash is a miracle. Bizarrely, when he stumbled out of the wreckage, he tried to make a run for it, but he was so drunk he fell over in the middle of the road and passed out." Ignacio rolled his eyes as he recollected the incident. "Keeping that jackass out of jail, and the story out of the news, cost me dearly. I wouldn't wish that maniac on anybody."

Dominic wondered how anyone could cover up that sort of high-profile incident. A fleeting glimpse of Ignacio's intimidating teeth with those weird grooves convinced him that the director must undoubtedly be part of a powerful cartel with extensive ties to the police.

When Dominic opened his mouth to speak, Ignacio, sensing the inevitable question, put his fingers to his lips to hush the actor. "Best you don't ask."

Dominic duly let the subject drop and inquired, "Is there an oddball peculiarity about me, too?"

Ignacio chuckled. "Don't worry. You and Jay are nothing alike. What you bring to the role is raw, animal intensity. Your eyes glisten with emotion constantly. The viewer is squarely focused on you when other actors speak their lines. Did you realize that? People in the foreground could be conversing, yet the audience can't help but peer around those actors to see what you're doing. That's a sign of star quality. You have that, which is why I'm excited about this picture. I have the right actors in front of the camera to bring the story to life and the right crew who know how to capture those performances on a roll of film. Throw your heart and soul into this picture, Dominic. You'll remember this movie fondly, and everyone who watches it will remember your performance. That stepping-stone you talked about—this movie is it. No matter how small it seems, it will find an audience once we give it the extra gloss it needs. Wouldn't it be magnificent if the movie found a fan base that adored it? A cult movie can have a greater impact on a generation of filmmakers than a special-effects-laden blockbuster, a socially relevant snooze fest that wins an Academy Award, or one of those other prestigious awards given out to club members only." His lip curled in distaste over the words "Academy Award." It was not a prize he valued. "Those pitiful awards have no place in society. They carry significance, of course, but only in a monetary sense. Almost all awards help sell a product. They work better than reviews in terms of marketing. I wish it were not so. Nevertheless, there it is."

There was a twisted smile on Dominic's face as he imagined himself on the red carpet, collecting an Oscar.

"I want to put as much care and attention into this picture as possible," continued Ignacio. "I intend to leave behind something of worth that has longevity." He gave Dominic a supportive pat on the back. "Perhaps, later, we might find time to talk about my next picture. It's a dark satire with a rather disturbing undertone. A shocking, misanthropic movie that people will discuss for years to come. I think it has the depth and commercial appeal you're looking for. The part I have in mind for you is the despicable yet captivating narrator, Serge. It might well turn out to be the defining role of your career. Anyway, that's for later. We have plenty of time to discuss it in the coming weeks."

The prospect of future film work made him buzz with excitement. Ignacio had dangled a carrot, and of course, Dominic wanted a nibble. His agent had hoped for just such a scenario.

Dominic instantly forgot that he had hated every minute and every single take. The potential for tragedy, each time the clapperboard announced a take, had shattered his nerves, and he had hardly slept a wink since he had arrived in the country. All the same, he would willingly put himself through it all again for the chance to add another movie to his paltry resume. His hope was that he wasn't about to die for his art.

They say fame comes at a price, but that was one price he wasn't willing to pay. Unfortunately, terror and catastrophe were inevitable ingredients when Ignacio made a picture, and those who survived his filmmaking process viewed their movie part as a badge of honor.

Twenty

ON a quiet evening, as he stood outside his room, searching for the room key, he heard Sofía's voice in the hallway. She was slightly out of breath as if she had raced up the stairs to catch up with him.

"I didn't think your room was on this floor," he said, surprised to see her.

"It's not." She tilted her head, giving him a look that suggested he should know why she was visiting him at this late hour. A tall bottle of rum was in her hand.

He found his key card and fed it into the key slot. There was a soft click, and the little green light on the door panel came on. He pushed open the door and stood in the doorway, regarding her with inquisitive eyes. "Would you like to come in?"

"I would prefer it to standing in the hallway," she said, boorishly pushing past him.

The last time they spoke, she seemed somewhat cold toward him. Now, her mood had turned distinctly arctic.

She put the bottle of rum on the bedside table. Knowing Sofía's penchant for excellent wine, exquisite food, and expensive designer wear, he figured that Isla Ñ Rum must be an exceptional brand. He watched her take off her jacket, draping it over the back of a chair, and then sit on his bed and cross her legs. There was an air of impatience about her while she sat stiffly, watching him close the door and hang up his sweater.

"For God's sake!" she growled as he emptied his pockets and put the various items on the bedside table next to the rum. "It takes you so long to do the simplest things?"

He kept his face averted, trying to hide his amusement. Evidently, he had done something to rattle her cage at some point earlier in the day.

"What did you want to talk about?" he asked, sitting beside her on the bed.

"What have you been telling Ignacio about me?" she said accusingly.

"Why on earth should I be talking to Ignacio about you?"

Her eyes narrowed. "Don't play the fool, Dominic. One of the crew overheard your conversation with him."

"I've had many conversations with him."

"I know," she responded moodily. "You've been chummy all week."

"What of it? You feel left out?"

"No. I just feel used and discarded. Like I've been stabbed in the back by someone I thought of as a friend."

"What the heck are you on about?"

"You know full well. You were talking about me today with Ignacio. It wasn't flattering."

He gave a dismissive wave of the hand. "Your eavesdroppers heard wrong."

"Ignacio has been discussing his next picture with you. Are you going to deny that?"

"Frankly, I don't see that it's any of your business."

"It *is* my business. Ignacio wants you to be the lead, and *I* was to be the lead actress."

He shook his head. "You're mistaken."

"When Ignacio spoke to you about his future project, you poisoned him against considering me for the part."

He sighed. "Your spies have it all wrong."

"When asked if I would make a good Penelope, you said you

liked the idea of Giselle Padlon."

Dominic's jaw tightened. He had indeed had a conversation with Ignacio about the movie and the main characters earlier in the day, so she had gotten her facts correct in that respect. As for being considered for one of the lead parts, Ignacio was undecided about whom to cast as Penelope. Nevertheless, when asked for his opinion of Sofía, Dominic hinted that Giselle Padlon might be a superior choice.

"I enjoyed Giselle's performance in *Monde de filles et de plaisir*. Based on Ignacio's plot outline, I think she would make a terrific Penelope."

"But he was considering *me* for the part!" she hissed.

Dominic smiled patiently. "He didn't make it clear. When we talked about the movie, he kept getting sidetracked. He asked me about all sorts of things that were completely unrelated. At one point, your name came up. I gave my opinion, and then he asked me about other actresses. I said what I thought of them, too. Then I happened to mention Giselle Padlon, who played a similar type of shady woman in *Monde de filles et de plaisir*."

"How very thoughtful of you," she retorted petulantly.

"I like to be helpful," he said with a goading smile.

"It would be helpful to *me* if you sang *my* praises rather than a stranger's."

"I was asked for my opinion, and I gave it," he said coolly. "I don't see why I should have to lie to him just because it suits you."

She chewed her lip, avoiding saying what was on her mind. After managing to swallow her anger, her face softened. "I was under the impression that we felt the same way about each other. Didn't I tell you before that we had chemistry? You agreed with me at the time. Or was that just a ploy to get me into bed?"

He avoided answering the question by saying, huffily, "What has that got to do with anything?"

"Do you think I'm a good actress, Dominic? I'm very versatile, don't you think? Wouldn't I be a good fit for the part?"

"I'm sure you would be very adequate," he said, attempting to get off the bed.

"Adequate!" she responded indignantly, banging her hand on his knee. "You're suggesting that Giselle is a better actress?"

"Not at all," he lied, jerking his leg free.

He succeeded in standing up despite her efforts to stop him. Then he moved briskly across the room to the wardrobe, reaching for his sweater. "I think I'll go to the bar for a nightcap."

She swiftly got to her feet and walked over to him. Her hands shot out, palms thudding into his chest, shoving him against the wardrobe. "Think you have what it takes to seduce Giselle, huh?"

He didn't respond, keen not to provoke her further.

She glared at him. "I know all about her. You're not her type. She likes her men bigger…tougher."

"Ignacio hasn't offered me the lead. We were merely discussing the movie, that's all. It wasn't a business conversation, just a chat."

"When a director discusses his next picture with an actor, it's a business conversation," she growled.

"When I see a contract, that's when he's decided he wants me for the part."

She let go of him. "Clearly, I didn't make myself understood when we talked about Ignacio all those weeks ago. I've worked with him for years. Over that time, we've built up a strong working relationship."

Dominic was aware of the sort of relationship they had, having heard stories about Ignacio's protectiveness. The man seemed to own her, dictating what acting parts she took and the people she saw. He assumed Ignacio must be aware of Sofía's recent indiscretions. She had fooled around with quite a few men since filming began, Dominic being one of them. As far as Dominic knew, Sebastián and Sofía were still an item, though she might have lost interest in the man since he had been demoted to his previous function of Assistant Director.

Dominic's throat tightened as he recalled the fate of the last actor who had engaged in hanky-panky with Sofía. Hadn't the jealous director stabbed him with a fork?

"He's directed me in television shows and commercials," continued Sofía, "and a music video. Now I have a big part in this movie. I owe Ignacio everything. I don't want that special relationship to come to an end. Do you understand?"

Her eyes flared with menace.

"Message understood."

"If there's a leading lady in his next picture, I expect to play that part."

He pulled open the door to the wardrobe, snatched his sweater from the hanger, and hurriedly put it on.

"I think you should tell Ignacio that you think I would make an excellent Penelope," Sofía told him, not dropping the subject.

He eyed her cautiously, calculating an escape route. "I'm sure he knows that already."

She put a hand on his chest to halt him. "Perhaps he needs reminding."

"It might be better coming from you. Ignacio already knows your attributes, and, after all, you can be very persuasive."

"He hasn't spoken to me about the picture. He would think it strange if I brought up the subject. I want *you* to do it."

"Not a good idea. It would look like I have a thing for you. I don't want to make Ignacio jealous."

"Then think of a suitable way to do it," she demanded. "Giselle might be offered that part instead of me, and it will be because of you. It's up to you to make it right."

"When we discuss the picture again, I'll remind Ignacio of your talents."

"Are you paying me lip service, or do you mean what you say?"

"Would I lie to you?"

She didn't like the way he said it. His sly smile was a distraction.

"Honestly, I don't know. I hope not, but the simple fact is, I don't know you well enough?"

He said caustically, "It wouldn't have been a bad idea if you had tried to get to know me better before now."

The candid remark surprised her, and she blinked at him broodingly. Then, in a cordial voice, she said, "Yes, I should have made an effort."

She immediately wrapped her arms around his neck and pressed her lips against his, thinking that was the smartest way to get to know him better.

He hoisted her onto his hips and carried her across the room, setting her down on the bed. She certainly wasn't without her charms, he reflected, getting to grips with her. Part of him wanted to work with her again, and part wanted to trade her for Giselle Padlon. Perhaps there was a way to achieve the two things, he wondered, hoping to convince Ignacio to audition them both.

Sofía hoped Dominic was smarter than he looked, but the mischievous glint in his eye didn't fill her with optimism. Her gaze shifted around the room, settling on the bottle of rum on the bedside table. She was dead set on getting that movie role and wouldn't forgive Dominic if his actions sabotaged her chances. As the lustful actor avidly pawed at her, she reflexively reached for the bottle, almost overwhelmed by a morbid desire to test the strength of the glass on the back of his head.

———— ✦ ————

Dominic was unclear how his character's final moments would play out on the screen, and despite a run-through beforehand, Ignacio had been deliberately vague about the scene's precise choreography. According to the script, Bruno, a pug-nosed police officer, secretly part of Silver Face's criminal outfit, deceives the main protagonist, luring him to a disused automotive manufacturing plant, allegedly to reveal incriminating evidence against a cabinet member. Having already exposed one high-level government official involved in arms trafficking, the fearless journalist then comes undone while attempting to bring down more of the country's prime figures of power. Although the audience already suspects a trap has been set, surmising from the policeman's shady behavior that he's a duplicitous character, Bruce Pucker is oblivious to the danger. He was a writer who would go to Timbuctoo for a lead story, and nothing excited him more than six column inches and a snappy headline. The surprise was not so much that he met with a grisly death but that it would be so graphic and unpleasant.

The moment Dominic stepped into the shadowy corridor, his throat tightened, and he felt an odd chill down the back of his neck. He strolled gingerly toward a set of drab gray fire doors, conspicuous worry lines on his face. The impending threat lurking beyond those doors was something he didn't want to contemplate. By now, he was familiar with the director's unscrupulous tactics for getting off-script reactions out of his actors. Dangerous stunt work, real effects, live ammunition…so far, he had put Dominic in peril without regard for his actor's personal safety. With the film nearing completion, there was no reason to suppose that the ensuing scenes should differ.

At the doors, Dominic hesitated, reticent to head through them. He was no method actor, and Bruce Pucker's fearlessness revolted him.

"Go on. The doors aren't locked," said the policeman gruffly.

"After you," Dominic insisted, half-turning to look at him.

Neither of these lines of dialogue was in the script, and Ignacio was happy to let the cameras keep rolling.

The actor playing Bruno suddenly seized Dominic, irritated that the actor had halted. With an angry growl, he shoved him hard in the back. Dominic stumbled forward with a muted shriek, his elbows slamming into the spring-loaded metal bar fixed horizontally across the center of the door. The door gave way at once, and he was propelled into an expansive stockroom.

Ignacio used a dolly shot, and the camera tracked the actor's lurching movements.

Dominic instantly confronted the director. His complaints about mistreatment were long overdue, but Ignacio undermined him, insisting that the scene-stealing supporting actors excelled in their roles. He said their pragmatic performances had resulted in Dominic's best work.

Ignacio backed up this opinion by showing Dominic footage of the previous scene. The cameraman had captured the antagonism quite wonderfully. Bruno's voice crackled with menace, his erratic movements intimating immediate danger. Though loath to admit it, Dominic now realized that Ignacio was right. The scene benefitted from the actor's physicality and unrestrained aggression.

During the next scene, however, Dominic had good reason to complain.

It began with him on all fours, surrounded by six burly actors dressed as policemen. They formed a circle around him, patiently waiting for Dominic to get to his feet, poised to strike. The sight of those surly faces would give him nightmares for months.

His left leg was shaky as he got to his feet, and when he heard the scrape of a shoe behind him, he tensed with fear.

The fear was warranted.

The hand that lashed out at his body was large and strong; alas, the novice actor didn't hold anything back. With careless vigor, he drove his tough, pointy knuckles into the small of Dominic's back. Dominic's legs buckled, and he found himself back on all fours, his body quivering with shock.

The director was peculiarly silent, gratefully observing this unexpected development with intense fascination. He still didn't make a sound when another of his reckless actors swung his foot at Dominic's head.

Dominic cried out in alarm and twisted away. The sharp kick

missed his nose by millimeters.

He couldn't dodge the next kick, which came at him fast, catching him hard in the chest. He was too winded and shocked to offer much resistance as the others set upon him with flagrant hostility, initially feigning to kick and punch him and then making contact with varying degrees of power. One of the actors gave the impression that he wanted to imprint the bottom of his shoe on Dominic's forehead. Another grabbed a clump of Dominic's hair in his fist and pulled him upright. Dominic was aware of the huddle of people surrounding him but couldn't clearly pick out a face among the throng of bodies. And then some good, study knuckles pounded against his head with robustness, and everything became a blur.

His eyes rolled up into his head, and all consciousness deserted him.

Twenty-One

WHEN he regained consciousness, he saw the director squatting beside him, patting a hand against his cheek. They weren't tender pats, either, but firm, insistent slaps.

"He's come to!" announced Ignacio.

Dominic regarded the man through slit eyes. The stubborn ache behind his eyes kept him from opening them fully.

"You took a slight blow to the head," explained Ignacio.

Dominic eased himself into a sitting position. Automatically, he put a hand through his hair, his fingers exploring the scalp for signs of damage.

"I was assaulted," he mumbled crossly as his fingers came across a lump the size of an egg. "I'm lucky my head isn't caved in."

Ignacio chewed his bottom lip, deeply embarrassed. "The actors got carried away. One of them hit you by mistake."

"That was no mistake. When you punch and kick somebody that hard, it's ABH."

"It was an accident," maintained Ignacio.

Dominic looked around at the faces of the actors. They hardly looked like actors, more like hired thugs. None of them gave him the impression they were sorry about what had happened.

"Where did you get these actors?" he growled. "The nearest prison?"

"Don't let the makeup fool you, Dominic. They are good people."

Good with their fists, certainly, thought Dominic, eyeing one of them skeptically. The man was conspicuously ugly, with cabbage ears and a cleft chin. There was a grisly scar down the side of his face that looked like it had been made by someone trying to etch their name into his skin with a broken beer bottle. Dominic couldn't tell if it was real or fake. It might be a clan face marking for all he knew.

"Let me help you up," offered Ignacio, taking Dominic by the arm.

The soreness in Dominic's back was brutal. The pain was nothing compared to his knees, which felt like somebody had taken a hammer to them. Ignacio let go of his arm, and Dominic swayed for a moment, trying to keep his balance.

"Are you ready to try for another take?" asked Ignacio.

The pained expression on Dominic's face gave way to a look of sheer disbelief.

"We'll take five," Ignacio told the crew, determining that his actor needed some recovery time.

Sebastián glanced apprehensively at his watch. "No more than five."

Dominic grabbed the director by his sleeve as the crew retreated and said firmly, "I'm done for the day."

Anxiety flashed through Ignacio's eyes for the first time. "No, that's not possible. We didn't finish the scene."

"Get a stuntman for the rest," said Dominic through clenched teeth.

"It won't work," argued Ignacio. "We need a continuous shot."

"The hell you do!" responded Dominic defiantly. "Nobody films a guy getting beaten to death for five minutes as a continuous shot. You can piece the scene together in the editing suite using the shit you already have."

"I need more footage. I need another take," Ignacio said despairingly.

Dominic stomped off the set, deaf to Ignacio's vitriolic threats.

He had been a punching bag for long enough and was beyond intimidation, apologies, rewards, or promises. He secreted himself in a trailer in the parking lot, staying hidden for much of the afternoon, forcing the director to rely on a stunt double to complete the torture scene.

When he walked back onto the set, he caught sight of the stunt double's swollen face and noticed bloodstains on the man's shirt. He looked like he had been in a prison yard brawl.

"How many ribs did they crack?" asked Dominic. "You still have your front teeth?"

Ignacio shooed the stunt double away, and then he turned to Dominic and growled, "Never walk off my set again."

"This production is a bloody death trap," raged Dominic. "I ought to sue. You bring in your thugs to take a pop at me, hoping one of them can break my nose and you can film it. You've no sense of time. We film all day and all night but still never get on schedule. You use live ammunition and dangerous props. You don't care about anyone but yourself and think you're making great art, but you can't tell a good take from a bad one."

Ignacio's mustache quivered, seeming to have a mind of its own. "That it?"

"No."

"Go on, then. What else have you got to say?"

"The script stinks, the extras look like felons, and I'm beginning to think that Jay Adler-Frankel was right."

"What did he say?"

"That you're a gangster. A no-good sonofabitch who's well-connected with crime syndicates. Your little posse controls Villa Española and Peñarol, as well as a bunch of other quarters."

"*Ese Bastardo*. I should have buried him when I had the chance."

Dominic's mouth opened, ready to let fly another torrent of criticism, but Ignacio's remark warned him against it. It seemed that Jay Adler-Frankel might well have been telling him the whole truth after all.

"I'm going back to the hotel," said Dominic.

He turned quickly, intending to pack his things and get the next flight home. His first day on the set had given him a good idea of how difficult it would be to get to the finish line. Jay Adler-Frankel had also given him fair warning. He could have been home by now, signed up with Ted Ferro, perhaps filming a picture in Hollywood. Instead, he had wasted nearly two months in Uruguay, trying to survive the director from hell.

Ignacio grabbed him and spun him around, saying, "You're not going anywhere."

The tone of his voice indicated he wasn't about to offer an apology for his behavior.

"I'm done for the day," insisted the actor.

His words lacked conviction. He wanted to run, but there was no Ted Ferro in his corner, available to answer his call and send a car. Bernie would give it a couple of days and then send a hearse.

"You arrogant youth."

"Hardly. I'm thirty-one."

"You drink all night and show up drunk to the film set every day. None of the actors have anything good to say about you. I've heard people call you *El Borracho*, the drunkard. It's a shock to people when you actually remember your lines. Doesn't happen often, unfortunately. You can't keep your hands off the lead actress. You lusted after her the moment you met her and seduced her within twenty-four hours of your arrival."

"My private life is none of your concern."

"It is when it breaches *my* private life. Your love scenes with Sofía should be staged here, acted out for the director, the cameraman, and the rest of the crew. There shouldn't be anything going on behind my back."

"She's not your property. There's no ring on her finger, nothing in the contract restricting other men from spending time with her off the set."

Ignacio prodded Dominic in the chest with his finger. "Touch her again, pal, and I'll mete out just punishment."

"Punishment. For what? Pleasing her?"

The man's finger shifted downward, poking Dominic hard in the crotch. "I will kick you so hard here you'll be singing soprano."

"That old line. We're done here."

The actor wriggled free, but Ignacio grabbed his arm again as soon as he attempted to leave. They scuffled for a while, grappling with one another like wrestlers, Ignacio perhaps looking for the takedown. He held the actor's arm firmly, trapping him, and for a moment, Dominic assumed the director was going into the turtle position. He twisted out of the move, avoiding the snap-down.

Ignacio lost his grip on Dominic's arm and growled, "Don't you dare walk off my set. You'll never make it to the hotel. We're in the home straight. The final weeks. You're not going to stall the production."

"Stall it! I'm leaving for good. I should have headed home weeks ago."

Ire erupted in the director's eyes. His elbow jerked back, and his fist slammed into Dominic's midriff. The wholly unexpected quick left jab to the solar plexus folded Dominic. He stayed on his feet, hunched over, wheezing noisily, unable to draw air back into his lungs.

Ignacio rested a soothing hand on Dominic's back as he became conscious of some of the film crew in the background watching his antics. "We'll take five," he announced to the shocked observers.

Then he leaned close to Dominic's ear and spoke in a low, hostile whisper. "You want to walk away from this movie? I'll have you buried alive."

He patted this actor gently on the back, resisting the urge to clobber him, and then casually sauntered away as if nothing had happened.

——■ ✦ ■——

Two guys who looked like linebackers escorted Dominic to his hotel that evening after filming was done for the day. Hotel security was put on high alert and informed that the actor shouldn't leave his room without an escort and that any attempt by the actor to leave the premises was to be deemed a crime.

The first night they locked him in his room, Dominic screamed for a bottle of Mac Pay Whisky and then threw a chair at the window. He couldn't break the plexiglass despite numerous attempts, so then he decided to trash the room. There wasn't much furniture to break, but he managed to make a good show of it. The way he threw his small refrigerator at the wall with Herculean force was something to marvel at, and he was sure the director would have loved to have gotten it on film. The thing was no longer a minibar but an empty chill box that was of no use to Dominic, so he destroyed it with malice and started looking for other things to kill.

The guest in the room next to him must have contacted reception to complain because, in the middle of his tantrum, one of his handlers burst into the room swinging a crowbar. He chased the actor around the room, stumbling over broken furniture and twisting his ankle. He screamed at Dominic, wanting to bludgeon him to death, but he wasn't able to whack the actor with his weapon, and a wild swing took out the ceiling fan.

A second thug emerged in the doorway, ready for the challenge. He rugby-tackled Dominic and got to work on the actor with his fists. The blows were good, and they kept the actor in check. They were body blows only that caused no fractures or ruptured organs. When he had finished, he got up, looking pleased with himself, saying, "Let me know if you want more."

The actor certainly didn't want more.

Soon after, he was moved to a different room, which had a

working ceiling fan and a refrigerator. However, the fact that it was empty made it just as useless.

Dominic was done with tantrums, and self-pity took over. He cried himself to sleep, weeping for a liquor bottle.

He was supervised constantly for the next week, his meals were brought to his room, and his handlers kept a careful watch on everything he did. The bar, he was told, was off limits, and so no alcohol passed his lips for seven consecutive days. It was the worst time of his life. His efforts at acting were pathetic. He wasn't conceited enough to suppose that his performance was noteworthy. He had the shakes. His body was a mess of bruises from the neck down. The light in his eyes, that dream of stardom, had been extinguished.

His career was still in its infancy, barely eight years out of the gate. It began with off-Broadway shows, and then, having moved to Los Angeles, parts in daytime television soaps and low-quality exploitation films followed. A succession of more prominent roles had teased him into believing he was growing as an actor, refining his talent, and preparing for the day when he would emerge as the leading man in a big production. Television, cinema, Broadway…the medium hadn't mattered to him. The essential element was the size of the billboard. Whatever the arena, he had been convinced that the major parts would come his way and that it was just a matter of patience. Thus, he had taken whatever came his way, wrongly assuming they wouldn't always be stinkers.

This latest motion picture made him think he must have crested at some point earlier. He didn't need to see the rushes to know it was an overworked piece of garbage and far from the breakthrough hit Ignacio was predicting. In fact, he had come to despise it, knowing it wouldn't do his career any good anyway. It was the stinker of all stinkers, possibly the tombstone in his career. That daft claim by Ignacio that it was a complex, multi-layered story with depth, vision, and artistic genius made him want to howl with laughter. Only he couldn't laugh. It was torture simply being here, suffering the clichéd bit of hokum. Every fiber in his body told him to do everything in his power to bury the film and ensure it wasn't finished or made public. The torture had to end; Ignacio's arm of power had to be shattered.

Dominic was sick of being a captive in Uruguay, a slave to the hood. *Ignacio must die*, he decided.

Twenty-Two

ÓSCAR Chiosso's reemergence in the final two weeks of filming brought about the sort of sudden, catastrophic change that only a man with his finely stewed militance could muster. When he strolled onto the set, wielding his metaphoric whip, Ignacio bristled at the sight of him. Hopes of a serene resolution to principal photography died the moment the two bullish men were within striking distance of one another.

The location this time was Piriápolis, a picturesque city on southern Uruguay's Atlantic coast that was once Uruguay's leading summer resort. The town, positioned around a curving bay, sported an Italian-style castle and age-old saloons. The eclectic historic architecture, which one could savor from a chairlift, included belle époque–style buildings, a blend of Victorian Gothic and Art Nouveau. The crew had set up their equipment at Piriápolis Beach, the most charming spot in town. Colorful striped beach tents and sun worshippers lined the golden sand, and the sumptuous backdrop comprised a vibrant green hill dotted with red-roofed buildings and an expansive esplanade stretching toward the flotilla of yachts at Piriápolis harbor.

"Cristian, let me see the daily call sheet," said Chiosso, approaching the Assistant Director.

He was wearing workman's boots rather than his usual moccasins, and the briskness in his stride broadcast that he was a man with a long list of tasks to accomplish and very little time in which to do it.

Sofía and Dominic looked up from their scripts, watching the executive producer's arrival with somber curiosity. Chiosso was not a welcome sight to any of the performers. Nonetheless, his presence intimated drama would follow.

"Good morning, Óscar," said Sebastián. "I'm Sebastián, by the way, not Cristian."

"Uhuh," nodded Chiosso. "And the call sheet? Where is it?"

Sebastián's face was full of apprehension, and it was now very far from being a good morning. He looked around for the Second AD, clicking his fingers frantically. "Ruben?!"

Among the sea of bodies around him, Ruben was nowhere to be found.

"Don't you have one?" said Chiosso impatiently. "For God's sake, Cristian. Give me yours."

Sebastián searched his pockets hurriedly and finally found his call sheet. He gave it to Chiosso with slight wariness. Previously, the executive producer's meddling behavior had been especially unhelpful. Other than his change of footwear, there was nothing about him to suppose things would be different this time.

Chiosso examined the call sheet leisurely, making little grunting noises as he looked at the various grided sections. "I saw the footage you shot when you took over from Ignacio," he remarked, not looking up from the sheet of paper.

"Oh?" said Sebastián, staring at him intently. For once, he was intrigued.

"Ignacio has built up a great reputation as an action director. He can pretty much pick and choose his projects these days. The country loves him," continued Chiosso. "His movie, *Policia sin Placa*, made me think he would be well-suited to this picture, but now I'm not so sure. Tastes change, and the moviegoing public doesn't always want the same formulaic movies year after year. Besides, the studio is eager to appeal to those beyond the country's border."

Sebastián continued to stare at Chiosso unblinkingly. As interesting as this was, he wanted to hear more about what the man thought of his directing skills rather than an assessment of Ignacio's market audience.

"Popularity aside, Ignacio's professionalism is suspect, isn't it? And what can we say about his time management skills? It sucks big time, right? He doesn't know day from night."

Sebastián was nodding in agreement. He suddenly stopped and looked around, fearful that Ignacio might have overheard them.

"After this picture, Ignacio intends to fly to Buenos Aires to discuss *Diez Dedos Que Matan*. The budget is small, and marketing and publicity will be limited, but the writer has written successful movies in the past. I've read the script; the dialogue is very good. I have a hunch that the studio might find they are sitting on a sleeper hit," Chiosso disclosed.

Dominic turned his attention back to his script, feeling that this was an unnecessary distraction. He noticed that Sofía remained swiveled in her seat, fully invested in eavesdropping their conversation.

"My gut feeling is that Ignacio is not right for the project," Chiosso continued. "His style is too blunt and macho. He will constrain the movie, targeting it to men in their twenties and early thirties. You have a more nuanced style, and I think that type of filmmaking will help this movie appeal to a broader audience."

Sebastián's eyes widened. He had never before been receptive to the producer's opinions, but hearing this thoughtful evaluation of his work gave him a newfound respect for the man.

"Ignacio's next movie is *Chilean Bullets*," divulged Chiosso. "It is another installment in his 'Bullet' series. It is the type of guys with guns movie that Ignacio is best suited to overseeing. I'm sure it will do well financially and appeal to his followers. I highly doubt it will draw new film lovers, though. His movies never come close to the watermark he set in the early Nineties. Anyway, my recommendation to the studio is that he be dropped from *Diez Dedos Que Matan* to focus fully on *Chilean Bullets*."

"Do you have somebody else in mind for *Diez Dedos Que Matan*?" asked Sebastián hopefully.

"It can be your first feature," Chiosso told him. "I will tell the studio that you are the preferred choice."

Sebastián's bleached teeth twinkled in the sunlight. He looked like he wanted to hug the executive producer. "This is very kind."

"What you deserve," Chiosso told him, giving Sebastián's shoulder a hearty slap.

"That's interesting," Dominic heard Sofía murmur.

The actor tried to concentrate on his lines, but the image of Sofía toadying to Sebastián was all he could think about. She would almost inevitably feature in *Diez Dedos Que Matan*, even if only in a small role. The movie business was all about connections, and Sofía never missed an opportunity to promote herself to those around her with the potential to advance her career. Sebastián was putty in her hands.

"Now, let's go through this call sheet," suggested Chiosso. "The timings look off to me. You had better explain the setups for this morning."

Dominic's eyes drifted away from the script in search of Ignacio. Chiosso's intrusive, hands-on approach forewarned him that things were going to get unpleasant rather swiftly. Ignacio was not a man who liked to be managed, and there was no time in the daily schedule for a series of mini-wars between the two sluggers. All he could hope was that he didn't find himself in the middle of their quarrels.

Some hope.

———— ✦ ————

Dominic strolled along the Rambla de los Argentinos promenade for the umpteenth time, believing he had finally mastered the art of walking hurriedly. Apparently, he was in denial mode.

According to Ignacio, his walk was lethargic and lacking control. Thirty takes later, Dominic still hadn't gotten it right.

"Cut!" Ignacio yelled once more, fuming.

He marched toward his lead actor, looking like he was about to kick the man in the ass.

"Every time I watch that jackass attempt to direct a scene, I begin to lose the will to live," Chiosso remarked to Sebastián. "He belongs in a straitjacket."

He watched the lunatic director prance around the waterfront promenade, demonstrating to Dominic the correct way to move his legs. The way the director marched his feet was ridiculous.

Chiosso turned to the AD. "How far are we behind schedule?"

"Three hours."

"What are the chances of getting all the scenes in the can?"

"At this rate, we'll be lucky if we get through half."

Chiosso shook his head wearily. "The guy is killing me."

"We're all suffering," Sebastián admitted.

Chiosso watched Ignacio for another minute and then walked away in frustration, unable to take it anymore. Sebastián could hear him on his cell phone, complaining noisily about Ignacio's behavior. His voice was full of vitriol, the words nothing but threats and demands.

Later, after the thirty-sixth take, Ignacio called for a ten-minute break. His cell phone rang repeatedly, and eventually, he answered the call. It was a call he wished he hadn't taken, and the outcome wasn't pretty.

Immediately, he marched over to Chiosso with a baleful face and waggled his index finger threateningly.

"What have you been telling Carlos?"

"What business is it of yours?" responded Chiosso.

"Nobody is firing me," insisted Ignacio. "I'm not going anywhere."

"The studio heads want to be rid of you, pronto? Is that what you're saying?"

The threatening finger was jabbing the air again, warding off Chiosso. "I'm not going anywhere, you hear."

"Did you explain that to Carlos?"

"He's not replacing me. That's what I told him, and that's how it will be. Stop stirring up trouble, damn you."

"You do that well enough yourself."

"This is *my* picture and mine alone. Carlos understands."

———— ✦ ————

At the end of the day, with the crew well behind schedule, logistics were a mess. They were committed to filming all over Montevideo and the surrounding towns and cities, requiring plans to be canceled and new daily call sheets drawn up. The shooting schedule for the penultimate week changed by the hour. Ignacio couldn't police himself and wasn't willing to speed up or accept an imperfect take. Everything had to pass his impossible merit scale.

Chiosso's biggest gripe was that the director was burning through hours and hours of expensive film, costing the studio unnecessary money. The daily rushes didn't inspire him, and he told everybody that Ignacio could no longer tell the difference between a good take and a bad one.

When the production returned to Montevideo, everyone was on edge, pressured by the long days and the lack of progress. Dominic tried his best to mask a nervous twitch. In point of fact, he was spiraling toward a nervous breakdown. Exhaustion and alcohol withdrawal were making the final days a tough slog, but his resentment toward Ignacio had reached a crest. He couldn't look at the man without feeling an overwhelming urge to slide a sharp knife into his gut and twist the hilt. The man's unyielding criticism of everything he did broke his spirit. He wasn't even sure if he understood the basic mechanics of acting anymore. His delivery was off, his way of listening to his fellow actor was deficient, and the way he moved and gestured was so artificial that he might have been better off working as a mime. Clearly, he wasn't suited to the movies or the stage or even amateur theatre. Nobody wanted to be part of the movie anymore, but Dominic didn't think he could actually make it through another day of filming.

Everything came to a head during a mid-week morning, with ten days of principal photography remaining. Unsurprisingly, Óscar Chiosso was the culprit.

The opening take involved the character María arriving at her rendezvous with Bruce Pucker, and Ignacio wanted to feature one of the city's most impressive attractions in the background— the eye-catching fifty-six-foot bronze statue of Uruguay's greatest national hero, Jose Gervasio Artigas, riding a horse. Artigas was a soldier and revolutionary leader who fought for equality and democracy. Underneath his monument was a mausoleum containing an urn with his ashes, guarded twenty-four hours a day by two honor guards. Believing that the monument was an appropriate meeting place for the two characters, Ignacio invested much of his time and energy in making the shot possible. He needed the assistance of the city police to cordon off sections of the Old Town, and he brought in hand-picked extras and a choreographer to work with them so that the crowd ebbed and flowed around the main actors in a satisfying way.

The great challenge for everyone involved was recreating the clearly defined vision Ignacio had in his head. He was such a stickler for capturing the shot just so that it became difficult to please him. They filmed take after take but to no avail. Something always seemed to mar the shot.

Chiosso finally lost patience with the intractable director and stormed onto the set, bawling, "You stubborn bastard! Just film the damn scene and print the best take!"

Ignacio shooed him away, gesticulating furiously. "The scene isn't right. Get off my set! And for God's sake, stay off it!"

"Carlos warned me about you last year and said you had temper problems. He didn't tell me the half of it. You're on the verge of cutting your own ear off."

"Why don't you cut yours off first. Better yet, rip out that foul tongue of yours."

"The trouble with you, Ignacio, is your perfectionism. You would spend two days trying to work out which part of the blade to use. You're a total waste of space. Your resume has ten completed films on it, but I don't see how the hell that's possible."

"There's a lot you don't understand."

"I understand that I made a big mistake persuading Carlos to hire you. You're on a mission to bankrupt the studio. This picture is so far in the red that it's beyond salvation. Don't you understand? The marketing budget will be zero. It's a dead loss."

"My foot is about sixty seconds away from kicking you across the street," warned Ignacio.

"You're a lost cause," Chiosso told him. "You couldn't manage a lemonade stand."

"Let's get one thing straight: I'm in charge of this picture," explained Ignacio in a voice that reverberated across the street. "You understand nothing of movies; you have no place on a movie set. Get out of here. I don't need your input and don't want it. I just want you off the set, out of my way."

"You keep tripping yourself up, Ignacio. You're your own worst enemy. I'm here to oversee this whole debacle," explained Chiosso. "I'm trying my best to keep the movie on track, but hell…it's impossible. I've asked Carlos to have you replaced for the picture *Diez Dedos Que Matan*."

"You did what?" Ignacio's skin tone turned eerily red, and his mustache quivered uncontrollably.

Chiosso turned to Sebastián. "Your name's Cristian, isn't it?"

"Sebastián."

"You'd better take over as director on this picture too."

Sebastián stared at the producer as if he had been asked to gnaw off his own toes.

Chiosso said crossly, "Well? Do you want to take over or not?"

"You're asking me to direct *this* picture?"

"Yes, dammit! Unless you'd rather direct traffic."

The distress in Sebastián's eyes made Chiosso regret offering him the job. He looked around for another viable candidate. The tip of Ignacio's shoe then struck him hard between his butt cheeks, lifting him off his feet.

Ignacio had landed it well, but nobody was applauding. Everyone looked mortified by his actions.

Chiosso turned and grabbed Ignacio by his shirt collar, but he didn't get the chance to yell and swear. Ignacio's knee automatically came up, thumping Chiosso in the crotch with satisfying force.

The man dropped onto one knee, wheezing noisily and clutching his privates. Ignacio then drove his fist into the man's neck, causing Chiosso to stoop like a man in prayer. The smarting ache in his groin was so fierce he was unable to remove his hands from his groin. He gritted his teeth and tried to ride out the pain.

Ignacio crouched down and put his lips close to Chiosso's ear. "Go home and recuperate. Put some ice on your swollen ego."

Chiosso struggled to his feet, clutching at Ignacio's shirt for support. He was pale-faced and watery-eyed. With great effort, he regained his balance and looked Ignacio in the eye.

"You're evil," he rasped.

His arm moved abruptly, the palm of his left hand striking Ignacio hard in the face. The blow knocked Ignacio sideways, and if Chiosso hadn't had a firm grip on his shirt, the director would have lost his footing completely.

Ignacio reeled with shock. The open-handed slap had caught him completely unawares; he had scarcely seen the man's arm move. Moreover, he couldn't recall the last time anyone had hit him. It was unthinkable and unforgivable.

Chiosso wasn't finished. People in his industry didn't communicate with their fists. In fact, his status was such that, generally speaking, people knew better than to get on his wrong side. He needed to land a few more strikes to restore his pride.

Ignacio handled Chiosso's right cross better than expected. The subsequent straight right nearly floored him. Chiosso's short right didn't have much effect, and Ignacio recovered in time to block the over hand right. It wasn't Chiosso's best combination of punches, and the truth is, it wasn't nearly good enough.

With a livid roar, Ignacio dropped his shoulders and charged at the producer, catching him in the chest and ramming him like a bull. He managed to lift the man off his feet and send him sprawling into the road.

Ignacio then thrust his hand into the thigh pocket of his rye-colored Cargo pants, cursing Chiosso in Spanish. There was savagery in his eyes, and he could barely contain his anger. His hand emerged from the pocket clutching a Smith & Wesson Model 642 revolver.

"Jesus Christ!" gasped Chiosso at the sight of the weapon.

The crew had been watching the ugly confrontation with hushed alarm, unwilling to interfere and incapable of providing requisite assistance. At the sight of the firearm, there was a collective gasp. Those closest to the producer made a sudden move to get away.

"Hold up your hands," demanded Ignacio. "I'm going shoot your nasty fingers off."

He released the safety and took aim.

"Oh, my God!" shrieked Chiosso, scrambling to his feet.

The gun erupted and a bullet whistled past Chiosso's head. He gasped and stumbled sideways, partially avoiding the second shot, which clipped his arm, spraying blood onto the stonework.

Chiosso screamed in pain and clutched his upper arm. His face was ashen, and his legs almost gave out on him.

Then he saw Ignacio's finger close on the trigger once more.

Twenty-Three

HE leaped out of the way as the gun exploded. The bullet sailed past him, crashing into the base of the Artigas Mausoleum monument.

The color drained from Dominic's cheeks as he saw Chiosso hit the ground clumsily and put his hands over his head, whimpering in Spanish.

A single scream echoed across the street, and then a wave of voices invaded the silence, with people shouting in fear and confusion. There was a blur of motion as watchers quickly fled the area, and some of the crew members took cover.

A voice behind Dominic yelled: "*El va a matar a todos!*"

The actor was so shocked by what had just happened that he was fixed to the spot, dumbly watching the film crew scatter, slowly processing the crazy situation and the need to seek shelter. He couldn't quite believe his eyes, and he didn't want to think that he, too, might actually be in genuine danger.

He looked for the cameraman, as if by some miracle this might be a scene in the movie, and realized it was far from being a scripted moment. The bodies, pushing past him, drew him into action, and as his feet began to move, driving him forward, the lumbering camera operator got in his way. Dominic watched him crash into the director of photography and then fall on his ass. The boom mic dropped to the ground, and the operator raced away, and then a frantic man behind Dominic screamed, "Run!

Protect yourselves! Clear the set!"

Dominic's frightened eyes darted back to the prone figure of Chiosso, who lay face down in the street in precisely the same spot where he had collapsed. He was panting noisily, fighting to control his fear, his hands still clamped tightly over his head.

Ignacio's arm suddenly moved, and Dominic saw the demented look in his eyes, hatred carved into his features. This wasn't merely a case of foolish hotheadedness; the man had cold, hard fury at his core. He wanted vengeance—to obliterate the overbearing producer from the planet. Bold, brutal, bloody reprisal for undermining his authority.

Ignacio trained the pistol on the wretched, cowering man, disgusted by the sniveling sounds emanating from him. The thought of letting Chiosso walk away with only a scratch was too much to bear. A bullet in the wretch's back was inadequate punishment, too. Ignacio craved harsher justice.

The small muzzle now pointed at the man's head. It was a big, bulbous target, so Ignacio wasn't likely to miss at this range. Soon, revulsion gave way to excitement as he visualized putting two bullets through Chiosso's skull and decorating the ground with his brains. Exhilarated by thoughts of the nasty mess he was about to make, his finger moved to the trigger with eagerness. He thought it a pity that the cameraman hadn't stuck around to record this momentous occasion. Ignacio was about to create beautiful art that would haunt the minds of his film crew for the rest of their lives.

Dominic was within ten feet of Ignacio, closest to the madness. Everyone had vacated the immediate danger zone, and the police were nowhere to be seen, leaving Dominic the prime witness to the atrocious assassination and far enough away from Chiosso to avoid getting splattered with blood. His heart skipped a beat as he watched Ignacio pull the trigger.

There was a soft click, followed by another one. Ignacio cursed and opened the cylinder on his Smith & Wesson. All the chambers were empty. He quickly pulled a handful of rounds from his pocket and started loading the chambers. It was anyone's guess where those five live rounds would end up. Were they all for Chiosso, or was that sick, sadistic swine about to turn the gun on other members of the crew? And where would it end? Would he spare a bullet for himself?

Without a moment's thought, Dominic sprinted at Ignacio, self-preservation rather than heroism fueling his actions.

Ignacio pressed the cylinder shut and took aim but didn't get his finger to the trigger in time. Dominic lunged at him, catching his right wrist with his left hand, forcing Ignacio's hand upward. The gun pointed skyward. At the same time, the palm of his right hand connected with Ignacio's chin, whacking the man hard on the jaw and pushing his head back.

The gun barked noisily, triggering the gaffer to let out a bloodcurdling scream.

As the bullet soared harmlessly into the sky, Dominic and Ignacio tumbled to the ground in a violent embrace. Their momentum carried them across the plaza in a tangle of limbs, rolling as one. The gun bounced twice on the ground and came to a stop in the middle of the square.

Ignacio recovered almost immediately despite clonking his head hard on the concrete, which served to terminate his angry yells. He shoved Dominic away and struggled to his feet. Though slightly dazed, he looked eager to tear someone's head from their shoulders and stamp the skull to smithereens.

While he staggered in the street, trying to focus his eyes, Dominic scrambled to his feet, grabbing hold of the director before the man could do further harm. But Ignacio's murderous rage hadn't entirely expired. He swiveled and struck Dominic full in the face with a meaty fist, the knuckles bouncing off the actor's left cheekbone with considerable force. Remarkably, the hefty blow didn't cause him much injury, although the way Dominic screeched and threw his head back, crew members watching from a distance were convinced that the handsome actor's facial features had been horridly rearranged.

The subsequent elbow to Dominic's ribs doubled him over, and then the enraged director slammed his forearm down on Dominic's back with all his might, sending the actor sprawling to the ground.

Somehow immune to the bruising treatment, Dominic grabbed Ignacio's ankle when the director moved for the gun. The director stumbled and fell, his face meeting the hard concrete with jarring force. Then Dominic dived onto Ignacio's back, pressing down on the man's kidneys with his knees and pinning him to the ground.

"*Quítate de mí!*" roared Ignacio, squirming.

Dominic pressed down on him with all his weight, refusing to budge. Although Ignacio struggled, determined to wriggle free, he couldn't force Dominic off his back.

Eventually, Dominic felt a hand on his right shoulder., and when he looked up, he saw three police officers gathered around him.

"We'll take him," one of them said.

Dominic climbed off Ignacio and stood back, watching the officers handcuff the famous director and escort him to the police car across the street.

"*Ay dios mío. Acabas de salvar la vida del productor!*" said the gaffer, staring at Dominic in disbelief.

"You just saved Óscar Chiosso's life," the camera operator translated, approaching Dominic excitedly.

Chiosso was on his feet, tears streaking his cheeks. His legs were weak, and he was struggling to stand. He was staring intently at Dominic, his face unable to settle on an appropriate expression.

The word that formed in his mouth was "*Héroe.*"

———■ ✦ ■———

The ringing telephone on his bedside table brought Dominic out of his extended sleep. "Hello?" he said groggily into the receiver.

"Dominic, that you?"

"Yes, Bernie, it's me."

"Thought I'd check in on you. See if anyone has succeeded in murdering you yet."

Dominic pulled himself into a sitting position, letting out a horrid, rattling cough.

"Christ! You sound dreadful, kid. Should I call reception and get them to send a doctor? Maybe we should also get the coroner on standby."

Dominic tried to ignore the nagging ache behind his eyes. His heavy drinking the night before, to calm his nerves after the anarchic spectacle in the Ciudad Vieja quarter, had wreaked havoc on his body. He was struggling to motivate his lips to move.

"No, I'm fine," he said hoarsely.

"A priest, then?" persisted Bernie. "You might want to consider offering up that deathbed confession now."

"What are you talking about?" He pressed his thumb and forefinger to his eyes to try to stabilize the pain behind them. It felt like a rodent was gnawing at his eye sockets.

"Hold on, Dom. I'll go make some popcorn. I'm sure you have a lot to confess, and this could get interesting. Hopefully, it will be more entertaining than your last god-awful movie."

Dominic squinted at the digital alarm clock on the table. It was ten o'clock in the morning. "You know I don't get up before noon on my rest days."

"I wanted to catch you before you went out for the day, prob'ly to hit up all the bars and the brothels in town."

"What is it you want?" said Dominic irritably, somehow managing to resist the urge to hang up the phone.

"I heard all about your thuggery on the set yesterday."

"*My* thuggery. You know damn well what happened. I'm hardly the villain. Hero, more like it."

"Everyone is in shock, Dom. According to Jules, that is. They can't believe you took down the Godfather and lived to tell the tale."

"The Godfather. Is that what they're calling him? Is he part of a syndicate? Exactly how high up is he?"

"There a severed horse's head in your bed?"

"No."

"Then he's probably not so high up. Either way, count yourself lucky he didn't put a slug in your kneecap."

"I can't wait to get out of here, Bern. This whole experience has been a disaster. Word is that the film has been shelved indefinitely. All my work was for nothing, and if I stay here much longer, I'm damn certain that the director's hoodlum pals will put my feet in cement and drop me somewhere in the Río de la Plata."

"I sympathize fully, Dom," Bernie declared. "I sent you out there. I'm partially to blame. All the same, I'm not entirely convinced that you don't deserve a Mob-style burial at sea."

"What are you saying?" said Dominic, appalled by his agent's honesty.

"Crazy rumors were flying about that Ignacio wanted to cast you in his next film. Screwing his woman behind his back and making an absolute ass of yourself put paid to that."

"How do you know that?"

"So, it *is* true!" The vicious growl in his throat gave Dominic a good idea of just how tightly his agent wanted to fix the noose around Dominic's throat. "Ignacio's personal assistant mailed me a film script about a week ago. That psycho director was keen to cast you in the central role. And then I got a fax a few days later that you were no longer being considered for the part on account of you schtupping the leading lady. He made it sound like she was his ward. Maybe also her pimp. Anyway, you totally botched the relationship, Dom, and savaged any chance of further collaboration."

"Does it even matter?" snapped Dominic. "He's been arrested. There wouldn't have been any future collaboration anyway."

"All the same, you can't go around burning bridges. I hoped you would network while you were out there, not antagonize the country's most famous director and get involved in real-life shoot 'em ups. Christ! You're worse than Jay Adler-Frankel."

"So, what now?" asked Dominic. I'm out of work and in an unsafe environment. I plan to get on the next flight out of here. But is there any work to come back to? Is there a quality script on your desk, Bern? I'll take pretty much anything."

"I don't know, Dom…"

"There must be something. Please, throw me a bone, will you."

Bernie cackled meanly. The misery in his client's voice delighted him. "There is something I've been holding onto, but it wouldn't interest you."

"Try me."

"It's an independent movie titled *El Asesino de Cholitas*. It's set in the Andean city of El Alto, close to the city of La Paz."

"Bolivia!?"

"You betcha."

"The script any good?"

"Best I've seen in a while. There's this group of fighting Cholitas competing in the ring, wrestling their way to fame and fortune. Eccentric bunch of mega-tough indigenous Aymara Indians who wear layered skirts, petticoats, and embroidered shawls. Sumo-sized broads, Dom, that like to toss men over their shoulders."

Bernie's enthusiasm wasn't contagious, and Dominic found himself wanting to decline the project. He waited for his agent to pause for breath so he could politely ask for something else.

"But their crooked manager is swindling them out of thousands of bolivianos. And there's this other whacko on the scene with a taste for Cholitas Anticucho."

"Wait. What? Are we talking tear-jerker or cookery show?"

"Slasher film."

"Huh?"

"There's a lunatic going around killing these fighting women, knocking them off one by one and cooking their remains. He's turning them into a dish called anticucho, a recipe originating in the 16th century in the Andean Mountain ranges. Bit like a Mediterranean shish kebab."

"Holy crap," murmured Dominic, now completely turned off by the project.

"Apparently, these Cholitas go great with potatoes and a peanut sauce."

"What else have you got?"

"That's it. Take it or leave it."

"I'll leave it."

"It's your call, Dom. If you change your mind, drop me a line, and I'll send word to the director about your fervent interest in her movie. I reckon you're a great fit for the part."

His baiting words reeled the actor in like he knew they would.

"What part are you referring to? The crooked manager? Is he the lead? Or are we talking about the serial killer?"

"A male wrestler."

Dominic's cremaster muscle contracted, pulling his testicles up into his body. "I should have known," he groaned. "You expect me to climb into a ring and take my chances with a gang of screaming female wrestlers. My God! I'd have better odds of surviving an avalanche."

"The director will see that you come to no harm. From what I hear, she dotes on her actors and protects them like members of her close family. She wouldn't let anyone harm a hair on your head."

Bernie cupped a hand over the mouthpiece on his telephone receiver and chuckled softly. He had heard some amusing stories about the director's scandalous behavior. She was a woman who loved men, especially young and athletic types. When people gossiped about her, the words that got bandied around the most were fanatical, covetous, insatiable.

"I'll think it over," lied Dominic. "But if something comes in—anything, really—please call me."

"Sure, kid. Oh, by the way, I heard a rumor the other day about a top acting agent. I suppose you'd call him a rival of sorts." He paused to blow his nose, deliberately making his client wait, consciously testing Dominic's patience.

"Go on," Dominic urged, his voice edged with concern. "What's his name? What's the rumor?"

"Ted Ferro."

Dominic's throat tightened. He felt his cremaster muscle contract again, and his balls winched into his body as if going into hiding.

"You've heard of him, right?"

Dominic acted like he had no clue who the man was, and of course, his fib was so hokey it wouldn't fool anyone.

Bernie cupped a hand over the receiver and chuckled some more. He was enjoying baiting his client. What he really wanted to do, though, was bash his client's skull in with the telephone receiver.

"Ted Ferro is a big cheese in the industry. Manages a lot of clients. I think Jay Adler-Frankel is one of them," Bernie mused aloud, feigning like he wasn't sure of his facts. "Unfortunately, Ted took a fall last week. Fell down a flight of stairs and broke both his legs. I hear he's in recovery healing nicely in hospital, but it might take a while before he's back at his office taking on new clients."

Dominic was suddenly eager to get off the phone. The news had shocked him. The fact that Bernie was telling him made him wonder if his agent could actually read his mind.

"Sounds awful, Bern. Thank God nothing bad has happened to you."

His agent stopped grinning and said sternly, "We'll discuss more when you're back in LA."

"Discuss work?"

"Your future."

He didn't like Bernie's tone of voice. There was a veiled threat in the words, a hint that Bernie was dropping him from his client list.

"Now go and have some fun," suggested Bernie. "Have a drink on me."

The reference to alcohol made Dominic's stomach gurgle. He had celebrated too much already, and the drinks were still repeating on him.

"Do you think…?"

The line went dead before Dominic got the words out. He replaced the receiver, feeling panicky about his future. His stay in Montevideo had made him question all sorts of things about himself. He was no longer sure what he wanted from life and what might make him happy.

He hadn't faced this career crisis before. Given that he was thirty-one years of age, he probably should have. Until this point, his entire focus had been on wealth and acclaim. The knowledge that Ted Ferro wouldn't be taking him on as a client anytime soon and that Bernie Finkelman might have plans to punish him for trying to dump him for a different acting agent made Dominic worry about what was in store for him when he returned home. What if his career was on the downswing already? What if he didn't land another acting part ever again?

He felt an abrupt tug at his intestines. It was as if someone was twisting a knife in his gut.

"You ever hear people say there's no such thing as bad publicity?" Bernie had once remarked. "Well, that's bullshit. Bad publicity doesn't do anyone any good."

Dominic picked up the telephone receiver, dialed the international prefix number, and then placed a call to his agent.

Right now, those in the film world in Latin America had associated his name with grit and courage, and the fact that the movie *A Bullet for Silver Face* wasn't rampaging across theater screens meant that nothing was corroding his positive image. While Ignacio was off the streets and the movie reels were gathering cobwebs, there was hope for him yet.

"What was the name of that Bolivian movie you were just talking about?"

Not The Dice Man's Cup of Tea
An Afterword by Nicholas Litchfield

LONG ago, my hopes of carving out a rewarding career as a pulp fiction writer took a bruising when I gave an early draft of a manuscript I'd just completed to George Powers Cockcroft. Better known by his pen name, Luke Rhinehart, George achieved fame in the 1970s with his novel *The Dice Man*. That book, his most successful by far, sold more than two million copies and was translated into twenty-six languages. When it first appeared in the U.S., its publisher professed that it was life-changing, and over the years, it's accumulated mind-boggling outbursts of hyperbolic declarations: named "one of the fifty most influential books of the last half of the twentieth century" by the BBC, *Time*, *Time Out*, the *Telegraph* and the *Toronto Star* elevated it to a lofty status, and the popular men's lifestyle magazine *Loaded* declared it "Novel of the Century." Its impact on entrepreneurs like Richard Branson and Jeremy King is well-documented, and the way it's motivated some to make crazy decisions dictated by the roll of the die is, frankly, alarming.

I was unaware of its effect when I first picked it up as a young adult. I found it, by chance, in a local thrift store and innocently began it soon afterward, rapidly becoming absorbed by the narrator's challenging, outrageous admissions. Ultimately, I was hooked, impressed by the lucid, enthralling writing, and unable to take a break, for 500 pages, from the central character's dice-living practices. I quickly read the sequel and the author's consequent books, hoping for something of similar merit. While nothing matched the brilliance of his debut, there are two that I consider well worth seeking out: *The Book of the Die*, an enlightening collection of essays, proverbs, and parables, and his overlooked gem, *Adventures of Wim*, which has a tenuous link to *The Dice Man*.

Years later, I stumbled across fresh titles when assessing the author's bibliography to see if he had written anything new. They looked new, at any rate. In fact, some were, and some weren't.

I looked a little closer at his publishing history and found that after 2000, he shifted his sights from traditional presses and entered the self-publishing arena. Using the big but expensive AuthorHouse, he produced four novels: *Whim* and *White Wind, Black Rider* (revised versions of books I'd previously read), and *Naked Before The World: A Lovely Pornographic Love Story* and *Jesus Invades George: An Alternative History* (two original novels). Given that he was once such a prominent author, I was intrigued by his decision to go this route. I don't believe it was the best choice, but it was in keeping with his general philosophy about getting his best work out there through whatever distributors and mediums were available.

Incidentally, by 2002, most of his books had fallen out of print, and I don't think he could bear them sinking into obscurity. His magnum opus has never been out of print, but I know he was frustrated that it hadn't been adapted into a motion picture. I remember asking him about director/producer Mark Waters, curious about the project status and if it would go into production. His response was discouraging: "Paramount has ended its relationship with Mark Waters' production company, and there has been no movement at all in the last four or five years on the script that Mark did with his brother in 2004." This would have been sometime in 2011. "That script, incidentally, contained not a single character or scene from my DICE MAN novel. Can you believe it?"

Obviously, he was relieved that the producer was no longer attached, and I can't say I blame him. Initially, Academy Award-winning John Schlesinger was assigned as director, but during the course of forty years, the project didn't move forward. Personally, I would have liked English filmmaker Bruce Robinson to have had a go at it. As a huge fan of *Withnail & I*, I couldn't imagine a better person to take on the task. I asked George what he thought, and he replied, "Bruce Robinson has certainly had an interesting career and done some good work. Do you know why he disappeared from filmmaking for a decade?"

I did—or at least I thought I did. Years earlier, I'd read a fascinating book-length interview with Robinson, titled *Smoking In Bed*, in which he confessed to giving up on movies for a long time because of his Hollywood experiences. Apparently, he had spent years trying to get funding for his comedy, *The Block*, but couldn't get it made. I'd assumed that this occupied his time for years, but in 2011, I was delighted to see he was attached to a forthcoming movie—*The Rum Diary*. He had been tinkering with the script, adding comedy where, originally, there was none, and he was currently filming it. I always felt that Hunter S. Thompson's novel, highly engrossing for the most part, fell flat in the last quarter. Turns out that Robinson's movie, which eventually surfaced a year later, would also fall flat in the final reel.

Though clearly interested in Robinson, George seemed to have his eye on a different director. "What do you think of Duncan Jones?" he asked.

The quality of *Moon* indicates he's a very capable filmmaker, and when you watch interviews and featurettes of him at work, he comes across as smart, likable, and good at getting the most out of his set designs. His rapport with the lead, Sam Rockwell, makes you believe he is easy to work with, which seems important. For what it's worth, I said as much to George.

I have no idea if Duncan Jones was ever attached to the

project. Did he express an interest? Was George considering approaching him?

Adapting *The Dice Man* to screen without disappointing its legion of hardcore fans feels like an unenviable task. Rewriting the entire story and casting aside all the characters and scenes from the manuscript hardly sounds like a sensible approach. Fortunately, a screenplay of *The Dice Man* already existed, one faithful to the original text. It was written by the book's creator—an adept screenwriter who composed nine screenplays, of which five were based on his novels, and two were straight *Dice Man* sequels. I have his finished draft of *White Wind, Black Rider*—he asked me to critique it, and I thought it was a wonderfully cinematic version of his book *Matari* and in need of no revisions. Unfortunately, none of these projects made it to the silver screen.

For the longest time, rewrites, film adaptations, and follow-on tales kept him from attempting something wholly new. That's my opinion. Even *Naked Before the World*, released in 2008, was an old work. He began it in 1969 while living in Deià, Mallorca, managing The Mediterranean Institute's study abroad program. The university would invite novelists like Anthony Burgess and Colin Wilson and famed poets like Robert Graves and Pulitzer Prize-winning Galway Kinnell to stay and give lectures.

Disappointingly, when I mentioned these four writers to George, curious to hear about his interactions and overall impressions of them, he claimed to have barely communicated with them. "I'm afraid I had no interesting interactions with any of the four writers you mention. I have always been more interested in an author's books than the author himself and made no effort to get to know any of them. So that aspect of my Deia years is a dead end."

He did form a friendship with Jay Linthicum, a young writer at the institute, and they collaborated on a novel. Publisher Mike Franklin acquired it, offering a modest advance, but later decided not to publish it. Eventually, George bought all the rights to the book from Jay, and many years later, he self-published it. It was a Swinging Sixties potboiler about sex and drugs that, I freely admit, I never found the enthusiasm to finish. Purportedly, someone had acquired the rights and was turning George's screenplay into a film starring Kristanna Loken. As with *The Dice Man* and its sequel, *Search for the Dice Man*, film developments ground to a permanent halt.

Novels aside, George sometimes dabbled in short fiction, although you'd be hard pushed to find his work in magazines. Humorous pieces like "Harry Meets God" and the little gems "SSSSHHHhhhhh" and "Bad Dreams" were freely available on his personal website, and even if he didn't often attempt short stories, he valued the medium. In fact, he became an early reader of the *Lowestoft Chronicle*, a quarterly magazine I founded in 2009, saying he thought it contained a lot of good writing and provocative stories. Though focused on travel, it had all types of stories, from mysteries, westerns, and speculative fiction to travelogues, high literature, and slice of life.

I invited him to submit work, and he was genuinely interested in having his stories appear in the quarterly issues, but he wasn't convinced he had anything that fit with the magazine's travel theme. Primarily, he was a writer of satirical and philosophical fiction, but *Long Voyage Back*, from the 1980s, was an apocalyptic thriller of nuclear war survival set on a sailboat that felt like something like that might work for the magazine. The question was, had he attempted anything else like that?

"I have written almost all my short pieces 'for the fun of it' and never tried to get any of them published," he admitted. "In some cases, I have actually rejected someone's wanting to publish a short piece because I didn't think I'd gotten it right. So it's possible I won't find anything I think is worthy of the Chronicle."

He never did locate a suitable piece.

As with his exploratory fiction, he was adventurous in life, too. He once sent me an interesting article he had just finished,

"The Dice Man, Deià, and Chance," which recounted his regretful purchase of a sailboat to cruise the Mediterranean and the perilous day the engine broke down on his catamaran, leaving him to brave stormy seas with the lives of his young family hanging in the balance. It's a reminder that a spirit of adventure can also spawn misery, despair, and humiliation. The article also explained how his influential first novel came to be published. While it's very readable and informative, part of me wants to hear about things unrelated to that manuscript. What about his teaching experiences in Deià and those other writers who came into his life? So much devotion to that one cult novel, but what about the others? "Were I to expand on the article you like, it would be by going into more detail about the writing of the book from the day it was first conceived in 1965 to the day I made my last revision, some time in 1971," he responded. "This would include more detail of the writing of most of the book in the spring of 1970."

While he may not have come up with a fitting story or travelogue that he thought would do justice to *Lowestoft Chronicle*, he did continue to read and enjoy the anthologies and the online editions, even touting the first print collection as an impetus for inspiring him to want to write short stories again. I like to think he enjoyed the later collection, *Intrepid Travelers*, even more, as he was complimentary of my interview with novelist James Reasoner and the caliber of the prose in general. He kindly wrote, "You should be extremely proud of the work you've been doing with the *Lowestoft Chronicle*. It's unique and, as the reviewer says, the quality of the writing is amazingly high."

Although we'd corresponded for years, we'd never actually met. So, when he emailed me, saying, "I'd love to have you come and visit us here next time you drive east past Albany on any occasion," I was greatly tempted to pack the car with a trunkful of his novels for him to sign and hit the highway. His substantial home was in Canaan, NY, which wasn't overly far from me, but I stupidly didn't take him up on the offer, not wanting to vacation from my beloved computer.

Sadly, he died in November 2020, nine days short of his 88th birthday. Regrettably, I didn't ever visit him at his home. I failed even to dial the telephone number he gave me.

As for that pulp novel I was working on…well, those aspirations of becoming a famous paperback writer in the vein of John D. MacDonald or Donald Hamilton, you may as well pound them to a pulp. Gentleman that he was, George let me down lightly. "I wouldn't have agreed to read your novel except that you told me it was short, and I want to help someone I admire and consider a friend." My story wasn't concise enough, and, friendship aside, he admitted that "it turned out not to be my cup of tea." He didn't find the characters engaging or original enough to hold his interest. In keeping with penny dreadfuls and the hordes of Dell Mapbooks, Gold Medal Originals, and Pocket Books that inspired me, the plot was lean, the dialogue terse, and the word count mercifully short—the manuscript was about the width of a couple of cardboard beer coasters stacked together. Nevertheless, getting through it posed a challenge for George.

"As a very successful editor, you've undoubtedly many times had the highly unpleasant task of telling a writer that the work he's submitted isn't quite up to snuff in your judgment," he wrote, likely with a heavy heart. "I know this will be a great disappointment to you as it is to me, but no sense being dishonest."

Disappointing, sure, but in point of fact, his candor was refreshing and necessary. Compliments are seldom given, and while nice to receive, critical observations offer the most value. Once the initial sting wears off, those negative comments provide a means for self-improvement. And that's what George's words became: a helpful reminder to work harder at establishing fresher, more interesting main characters. The type that crops up in George's early books. Thinkers, searchers, risk-takers.

Later, in the summer of 2014, I completed a brawn and bullets manuscript titled *A Bullet for Silver Face* about the making of a fictitious low-budget cult movie. The title, referencing the book's fictional film, ultimately became *When The Actor Inspired Chaos and Bloodshed*. Written in a matter of weeks, I edited it for months and pitched it to half a dozen agents without success. It got put away in a drawer, surfacing every year or two for a month at a time, only to gravitate back to the drawer and be forgotten while I worked on more pressing writing assignments.

Eventually, over ten years, I got around to pruning, cultivating, and preparing it for publication. Infuriatingly, the publication part always seemed a lifetime away. A reader would offer critical feedback whenever I deemed it finished, and so began more revisions.

Essentially, I have devoted ten years to editing a story that took me less than two months to write.

Despite the hundreds of hours invested and the years of rewrites, by and large, the plot and the characters remain unchanged from the original draft. In fact, the handsome but underwhelming actor and his vile agent are escapees from a different, much earlier novel, both morphing out of that project I was working on years earlier—the story that George struggled to like. I kept their bones and built flesh on them. I gave them new identities, placed them in new surroundings, and reimagined their look and sound.

George would not have recognized them—at least, I don't think he would—but would he have approved of them this time around? Would he have wanted to invest his time in seeing how their lives pan out?

"Most novels I try to read, I never finish," he divulged. "In my old age, I seldom find any novel refreshing enough to recommend."

I daresay that *When The Actor Inspired Chaos And Bloodshed* probably wouldn't have been his cup of tea either. The size of it alone would have dampened his spirits. And yet, I'd like him to have held the manuscript in his hands and felt its weight, perhaps turned a page or two. Surely, he couldn't have disliked it more than that other novel. Could he?

Either way, it doesn't much matter. George played his part when it was needed, and as a consequence of his critical feedback, he had a hand in forming these principal characters. I like to think it's a better novel because of it.